Francis Peacock Simpson

Latin Prose After the Best Authors

Francis Peacock Simpson

Latin Prose After the Best Authors

ISBN/EAN: 9783337370992

Printed in Europe, USA, Canada, Australia, Japan

Cover: Foto ©Andreas Hilbeck / pixelio.de

More available books at **www.hansebooks.com**

AFTER THE

BEST AUTHORS

PART I.
CAESARIAN PROSE.

BY

FRANCIS P. SIMPSON, B.A.

BALLIOL COLLEGE, OXFORD;
EDITOR OF 'SELECT POEMS OF CATULLUS', 'DEMOSTHENES ON
THE CROWN'.

𝕷𝖔𝖓𝖉𝖔𝖓:

MACMILLAN AND CO.

1885

CONTENTS.

PREFACE.

EACH group of these Exercises is founded on a passage of Caesar[1]. All the words, phrases and constructions needed for the translation of the English into Latin will be found in the specified portion of the Commentaries, and on the other hand all, or practically all, of the words, phrases and constructions to be found in that portion of the Commentaries are brought into use: these two conditions I felt bound to lay down for myself, as in no other way was it possible seriously to attain the end desired.

Everybody knows how many more Latin phrases he can translate into English than are at his command when he has to compose in Latin. It is desired, in the series of which the present is the first part, to try to reduce this disproportion, by making books, which are generally read for purposes of translation, serve also to increase the vocabulary for purposes of composition. At the same time there should grow a precise and definite sense of style, a practical and experienced ability to discriminate and imitate different styles. Of course neither the aim nor the method is new—both are as old, perhaps, as the first learner of a language not his

---

[1] I have confined myself to *Bell. Gall.* Bks. I.—VI., '*ut, si saepius decertandum sit,...semper novus veniam.*'

own: but I think teachers will be glad to have ready at hand exercises which may help to supply the necessary means. If these exercises often limp, as they often do, it should be remembered that it may sometimes have been hard to dance in the fetters necessarily imposed.

It will, at any rate, be an advantage to avoid the habit of depending on English-Latin dictionaries, a habit which, even if it were sure the dictionaries did not mislead, tends to make the composer helpless when they are not by. It seems likely, too, that what we draw for ourselves from original sources will show especially bright and fresh in use. A good Latin-English Lexicon, of course, can hardly be read too much, particularly if, according to the good old rule, 'when you look up a word, you read the article through.' But when we require, in composition, to pass from our own to another language, it is surely best

'vivas audire et reddere voces.'

The translation of each portion, and if possible of the previous portions, of the *Caesar*, must, obviously, have been thoroughly mastered, before a group of exercises be set about. At first a pupil may complain that the necessary materials are not to be found in the original. But all the exercises have been tested in practice, and so far is the complaint from being true, that there is often a choice of diction. Gradually he will acquire an almost unconscious habit of appropriating new and serviceable phrases as they are met with, and so adding to his stock, which will, each week, be remarkably enlarged by an almost unearned increment.

The exercises are graduated in difficulty : few will find the earlier ones too hard, or the later ones too easy. They may be begun as soon as the accidence and the more elementary rules of syntax are known ; in fact, as soon as Caesar can be read. The advantage of beginning continuous prose as soon as possible need only be named.

A note on the Subjunctive Mood, in special reference to the Conditional Sentence, has been inserted, because even good class-books[1] begin to explain the Conditional Sentence from certain usages of the Indicative—which is, surely, to take hold of the stick by the wrong end.

The note on 'Reported Speech' is absolutely necessary, as younger students must have constantly before them, for reference, a connected and tabular statement of its special forms, until familiarity shall have made them infallible.

[1] Even Professor W. W. Goodwin begins the account of the Greek Conditional Sentence with the example εἰ τοῦτο ποιεῖν δύναται, ποιεῖ: and does not hint at the fact that 'impossible conditions' took the Indicative form in Attic *by accident*. Comparative syntax shows that 'impossible conditions' required to be expressed in Greek by a past tense of the Optative mood. But Greek had no past tense of the Optative mood—as we are emphatically told by Curtius (*Elucid.* trans. E. Abbott, c. xx.) "that language possesses no other means whatever to denote past time generally than the augment." Hence either tense or mood had to be sacrificed: Homer sacrificed the former; Attic came to sacrifice the latter, though doing its best to make up the loss by means of ἄν or periphrases.

It is hoped that the note on Caesar's style may help to remove an idea, generally prevalent in the world of school, that the Commentaries are merely a dull exercise-book, and that to write Latin like Caesar is a puerile achievement. There would be more reason in a protest against degrading the Commentaries to a school-book : but we may infer "with modesty enough, and likelihood to lead it," that such "base uses" will always be made of "Imperial Caesar, dead and turn'd to clay."

FRANCIS P. SIMPSON.

KENSINGTON, *March,* 1884.

A Key is provided for the convenience of Teachers.

In class-work, it will be found a very good thing to translate the back Exercises into Latin *viva voce,* going over each two or three times, in order to acquire fluency; and, in view of this, the later Exercises increase in length. There is really no reason why a page of ordinary English should not be turned into Latin very nearly as fluently as a page of ordinary Latin can be translated by the same pupil. This, after going through the bulk of the present little volume—about two Terms' work with average boys— can, I have found by repeated trials, be done very well. In every case a considerable command of sound and idiomatic Latin is gained, most useful and indispensable for higher flights in Prose.

NOTES.

I.

THE MOOD.

THE term MOOD, like many other terms borrowed by us from the later Latin grammarians, and by them translated, or more often mistranslated, from the Greek, conveys little definite meaning to most minds. It has, however, chiefly in connection with the Latin Subjunctive, gathered a new signification which contains important truth ; though this is obscured by the continued application of the word to the Indicative forms of the verb, and—even in good books—to the Infinitive.

If we analyse one of the fullest Latin verb-forms belonging to the Indicative group, it will be resolved into root-element, verbal stem-element, tense-element, number-element, person-element, voice-element[1]. If we analyse one of the fullest verb-forms belonging to the Subjunctive group, it will be resolved into root-element, verbal stem-element, tense-element, *mood-element*, number-element, person-element, voice-element[2]. That is to say the Subjunctive has an additional element, found in no Indicative form. This is

---

[1] Thus :—

root-el.	*stem-el.*	*tense-el*	*number-el.*	*person-el.*	*voice-el.*
tol-	l-	eba-	n-	t-	**ur.**

Of course no theory is here intended to be advanced as to the origin or mutual relations of the elements -n- and -t-.

[2] Thus :—

root-el.	*stem-el.*	*tense-el.*	*mood-el.*	*number-el.*	*person-el.*	*voice-el.*
tol-	l-	er-	ē-	n-	t-	ur.

called the *modal* element. The new meaning of Mood,
then, is, that a mood-form possesses a certain significant
element not possessed by any other group of verbal forms.
In Latin such an element is possessed only by the forms
called Subjunctive. Latin has, in this sense of the word,
only one mood, the Subjunctive[1].

What, then, is the modal element? The comparative
method reveals that, in Graeco-Italian, there are two modal
elements, a and j (= i = y). These have been identified with
the roots of *Esse* and *Ire*. In Greek the presence of the one
or of the other chiefly distinguishes the one from the other
of the two Greek moods, which also differ in use and meaning. In classical Latin there is, for all practical purposes,
one mood only, formed by the presence now of the one,
now of the other element, sometimes of both. The force
of the modal element may be most conveniently expressed
as equivalent to 'think that,' 'suppose that'; that is, when
we use a modal form we mean to say that *we think, imagine*
or *suppose* the action of the verb, that the action of the verb
goes on in our mind.

The bearing of this on all the uses of the Subjunctive is
obvious[2]: we are here only concerned with two.

[1] Of course even a purely idiomatic accretion of meaning, without
the presence of a special phonetic element to bear it, would be enough
to constitute a Mood in this sense: but it seems a straining of the point
to retain the name Mood for Indicative forms because these have, perhaps,
got, by contrast with the Subjunctive, 'a sub-implication of fact.'

[2] For quite the best explanation of uses of the Mood see Roby's
Latin Grammar, Bk. IV.

I.

THE CONDITIONAL SENTENCE.

All true Conditional Sentences deal with what logicians call 'contingent matter,' that is to say 'things that may or may not be.' The protasis, or clause containing the supposed condition (which may be conveniently spoken of as the *conditional clause*), and the apodosis, or clause containing the supposed concomitant or result of that condition (which may be conveniently spoken of as the *hypothetical clause*), are the two halves of the whole Conditional Sentence, and each states something 'that may or may not be,' each deals with 'contingent matter.' How is the contingency to be indicated in each case? How can we show that we are supposing or conceiving the action of each verb? Of course, by using words to that effect, or, if not words, at least some significant sound-element which will give the necessary information.

We have seen that the modal element has a force and meaning which would be appropriate for this purpose; and in the languages belonging to our own family, in English[1] (though more plainly in its earlier stages), in Latin, Greek and so forth, the normal construction of a Conditional Sentence is, that, alike the verb in the conditional clause and the verb in the hypothetical clause should take the modal form.

---

[1] In such a sentence as '*Had* I the wings of a dove,' the 'had' is, of course, not a past indicative, but a modal form.

Generally, though not of absolute necessity, the force of the modal form—for all inflectional elements tend to lose their force—is eked out by particles. Thus in Latin the Subjunctive in the protasis is assisted by *si* or some equivalent: the Optative of the apodosis in Attic Greek is assisted by ἄν. The tense of the verb must, of course, be present or past, according as we speak of what is, or was, contingent,—of what may or may not be, or of what might or might not have been.

When we speak of contingencies as past, we imply that what might have been (or not have been) cannot now be (or not be); that is to say, past contingencies are present impossibilities.

'The gods themselves cannot undo the past.'

By a connection of thought which is quite natural, then, the Greeks and the Romans, and indeed we ourselves, express present impossibilities as past contingencies.

Hence we get the following

Schema of Conditional Sentences.

(1) Present Contingencies must be expressed in the Present tense of the Mood.

(2) Past Contingencies }
    Present Impossibilities }   ,,   ,,   ,, Imperfect ,, ,,

(3) Past Impossibilities   ,,   ,,   ,, Pluperfect ,. ,,

The only Latin exception to this Schema is that sometimes in (3) the pluperfect Indicative is found in the apodosis, as '*perieram, nisi subvenisses.*' This, of course, is logically an exaggeration, made for the sake of vivid effect. The Schema applies to other languages than Latin, though occasionally a language may lack the necessary verb-form, and may be obliged to substitute another verb-form or a periphrasis.

As a rule the tense in the protasis and the tense in the apodosis are the same, but sometimes one contingency is regarded as anterior to the other, and is therefore put a tense further into the past, i.e. into Perfect instead of Present, Pluperfect instead of Imperfect, Subjunctive.

The construction given above is, then, the normal construction. But people will not always speak by rule, nor always think in the old grooves. Sometimes we choose to regard a matter, not as contingent, but as sure to occur,— that is, we prophesy it, and, in Latin, use a future Indicative. But it is quite illogical to consider such sentences as belonging grammatically to the same class as Conditional Sentences, simply because they contain '*si*-clauses,' and Conditional Sentences also often contain '*si*-clauses.' The same remark applies to other sentences where *si* is used with a present or past Indicative. No Indicative forms, except the one mentioned under (3), imply contingency, which is the essence of the Conditional Sentence. They are statements or prophecies, with the protasis modified by means of the particle *si*. An Indicative protasis with *si* expresses, not *contingency* in *the action denoted by the verb,* but *doubt, uncertainty or ignorance* in *the mind of the speaker as to the accuracy of his statement;* it makes a statement 'with a doubt.' Hence the fact that we cannot combine an Indicative and a Subjunctive clause so as to form one whole Conditional Sentence. With regard to the *si* it need only be said, that, just as the particular meaning of a preposition is determined by the noun-inflection which it accompanies, so the particular meaning of a particle is determined by the verb-inflection which it accompanies: or that (according to what is nowadays not a paradox but a truism), as cases 'govern' prepositions, so moods 'govern' particles. Prepositions and particles are like the chameleons of legend and take their special shade of meaning from their surroundings.

2.

Another natural use of the mood is in reporting statements, made by another person, for the actual fact or truth of which the reporter does not vouch, but treats them as the thoughts or suppositions of the speaker.

NOTE II.

REPORTED SPEECH[1].

We may imagine a Minister to rise in a House of Assembly, and, addressing the President, to say :

[1] Examples, taken from Caesar, of all the following rules and Schemata, will be found in an Appendix at the end of the Volume.

"I do not think now is the time for us to dispute about your authority. This is a thing settled and established, not today or yesterday only,—an institution which has survived our fathers and will outlast my life at least. Are we not, is not every legislative body, bound to decide by a reference to traditionary policy what path to follow? Go on, Sir, in your course of integrity and dignity—why should you swerve? I do not believe, if I am asked my opinion, that such a thing is possible. Let us show ourselves worthy of you, our present director."

These remarks would probably appear in the next day's Parliamentary Report in a somewhat altered shape:

The Rt. Hon. Gentleman said he did not think that then was the time for them to dispute about his (the President's) authority. That was a thing settled and established, not that day nor the day before only—an institution which had survived their fathers, and would outlast his (the speaker's) life at least. Were they not, was not every legislative body, bound to decide by a reference to traditionary policy what path to follow? Let him (the President) go on in his course of integrity and dignity—why should he swerve? He (the speaker) did not believe, if he were asked his opinion, that such a thing was possible. Let them show themselves worthy of him, their then director.

If with the *quotation*, giving the exact words of the speaker, we compare the *report* of the speech, many changes will be found to have taken place of mood, tense, person, pronoun, and adverb. Similar changes would take place in Greek and other languages that belong to the same great family as our own, but in none are they more rigorously to be observed than in Latin.

A quotation is, in Latin, called 'Oratio Recta,' a report

'Oratio Obliqua.' The changes which must be made in passing from the former to the latter are now to be given.

The distinction between Subordinate and Principal Sentences is here all-important. It will be convenient to deal with Subordinate Sentences first.

A.   SUBORDINATE SENTENCES.

Subordinate Sentences may be roughly said to be such as contain a *definition* or *qualification*, introduced by relative adjectives (qui[1], quantus, qualis &c.), or by relative particles of time and place (cum, quando, postquam, qua, quo, ubi &c.), or by indefinite adjectives or particles (quisquis, quicunque, quot: quandocunque, quoties, quoquo, &c.); a *concession*, introduced by si, etsi, quamvis, quamquam, licet &c.; a *reason*, introduced by a relative adjective, or quod, quia, quoniam &c.; a *condition*, introduced by si, dum, modo &c.; a *purpose* or *consequence*, introduced by a relative adjective, or ut, ne, quin, quominus &c.; or lastly, a *dependent interrogation.*

In all Subordinate Sentences the verb must, in transition from Oratio Recta to Oratio Obliqua, be put in the Subjunctive[2]. Why the Subjunctive is appropriately employed here has been explained in NOTE I. When a Sub-

---

[1] It must be carefully borne in mind that *qui, cum,* sometimes introduce *principal* sentences, when they are equivalent to *et is* &c. *et tum* &c.

[2] For the few exceptions see Roby, *Lat. Gr.* Bk. IV. c. XXIV.

ordinate Sentence, in a reported speech, is in the In-dicative, it contains a remark of the reporter himself.

The verb will also take the third person : except where the reporter, or the person or persons to whom the report is made, happen themselves to be referred to in the speech— in the former case the first person (cf. Caesar's *nos, noster* of the Romans), in the latter case the second person, will be used in the Oratio Obliqua.

Also, the verb will naturally require to be placed in a past tense. The use of the Mood treats the speaker's statements as his thoughts or suppositions : when the speech is reported these thoughts or suppositions already, of course, belong to the past. Thus a present or future will become imperfect ; a perfect or completed future will become a pluperfect.

But we need turn over very few pages of the Gallic War to discover, in some of the reports of speeches which are given there, instances of the present and of the perfect Sub-junctive. This means that, for greater liveliness of effect, Caesar chose to regard the statements he reported not as past but as present thoughts and suppositions : in other words, he replaced the normal past tense by an 'historic present.' When this occurs the introductory verb is often itself an historic present : cf. *Bell. Gall.* I. cc. 8, 11, 14 *ad fin.*, 16 *ad fin.*, 17, 18. Not that this is always so. The introductory verb is in the past, yet the present, or more vivid construction, occurs in a speech reported in c. 44 *ad init.*; the introductory verb is in the present, yet we have, in the report, the normal past, in cc. 20, 35, 42, 47 ; and both constructions occur in the same report, cc. 7 *med.*, 14, 31, 40, 44. Probably the more vivid mode of expression is chiefly used to break the monotony of long reports in the normal shape. It is important however to remember that the use of the past tense is normal—that is to say, it is most usual in Latin and is common to Latin and the kindred languages. The present and past times must, of course, never be mixed in the same period. In the following Schema of Subordinate Sentences the less normal usage, though of course quite good Latin, is marked †, that it may be understood to require to be associated with the corresponding usage marked † in the Schemata of Principal Sentences.

SCHEMA I.

SUBORDINATE SENTENCES.

Oratio Recta.	*Oratio Obliqua.*
Present } Future }	{ Imperfect—sometimes { †Present—Subjunctive
Perfect } Completed Future }	{ Pluperfect—sometimes { †Perfect—Subjunctive
Imperfect	Imperfect Subjunctive
Pluperfect	Pluperfect Subjunctive
Pluperfect Subjunctive occurring in the hypothesis (apodosis) of a conditional sentence, when that conditional sentence itself is a dependent interrogation, or is introduced by a consecutive particle (as *ut* of consequence)	{ Future participle with { the proper person of { *Fuerim.*

B. PRINCIPAL SENTENCES.

A Principal Sentence may contain an affirmative or negative (α) *statement* only, (β) *question*, (γ) *command*, (δ) *wish*, or (ε) *hypothesis*, as in the apodosis of a whole Conditional Sentence.

α.

When a principal sentence contains a *Statement* only, the subject takes, in Oratio Obliqua, the accusative case, and if it be a pronoun should never be omitted, even though it may have been omitted in Oratio Recta—see, however, C below; the verb takes the Infinitive[1] form.

[1] This is a 'rule of thumb.' It hangs on a double assumption, that Latin has really a true perfect Infinitive passive and true future Infinitives, active and passive, quite parallel to the present Infinitives, and that Latin never really uses in main predication (oblique) any other save an Infinitive form. It would be strange if this were so, if Greek, for instance,—not to mention other languages—in spite of its much fuller system of Infinitives, should still use other constructions in oblique predication (for example, the participial construction, without, as well as with, the 'tag' εἶναι), yet Latin, having for its only Infinitives a present active and passive and a perfect active, should confine itself to one strictly Infinitive construction. It is more than probable that what are called the Latin future Infinitive active and perfect Infinitive passive are (whether with or without *esse*) examples of a participial construction; that instances can be adduced of the present participle similarly used; and that in the periphrasis known as the future Infinitive passive the impersonal verb is syntactically in a different case from the usual oblique Infinitive—*Dicit urbem captum iri* = 'He-speaks-of things-tending to-the-taking-of the-city' (*iri* used as accusative, not dative or locative, and *urbem* object to *captum*). But as the assumption mentioned

The employment here of the Infinitive requires a word of explanation. The Infinitive is a case of a verbal noun which has the peculiar faculty of admitting tense-elements. The meaning of the case-ending, in this usage, may be fairly stated as 'in connection with.' Hence *Dicit Caesarem venire* literally = 'He-speaks-of Caesar in-connection-with-coming.'

The correspondence of tenses between the finite forms in the Oratio Recta and the Infinitive of the Oratio Obliqua is given below.

SCHEMA II.

PRINCIPAL STATEMENTS.

Oratio Recta.	*Oratio Obliqua.*
Present	Present Infinitive
Future ⎫ Completed Future ⎬	Future Infinitive
Perfect ⎫ Imperfect ⎬ Pluperfect ⎭	Perfect Infinitive

Of course when verbs lack a future participle, as do Inceptives &c., *fore ut* or *futurum esse ut* must be used with the Imperfect Subjunctive, or sometimes the †Present Subjunctive.

above is made in all grammars, and is here convenient, it is retained for convenience sake. However scientifically inaccurate or inadequate the rule may be, it is not in practice, at any rate, in the least misleading; and grammatical heresy need not be breathed, unless it be not only true but profitable.

β.

When a Principal Sentence contains an *Interrogation*, a distinction must be made between (i) questions the subject of which is in the first or third person, and (ii) questions the subject of which is in the second person.

(i) Questions of the former kind, sometimes called 'rhetorical questions,' adopt in Oratio Obliqua the construction of accusative with infinitive.

But if the question was originally in the deliberative subjunctive, the subjunctive will remain—of course in the third person; and the tense will become past, except in the 'vivid' usage †.

(ii) Questions of which the subject is in the second person take the subjunctive, according to the following Schema.

SCHEMA III.

DIRECT QUESTIONS IN THE SECOND PERSON.

Oratio Recta.	*Oratio Obliqua.*
Present	{ Imperfect—sometimes { †Present—Subjunctive
Perfect	{ Pluperfect—sometimes { †Perfect—Subjunctive
Future Completed Future }	{ Future Participle with Imperfect—sometimes †Present—Subjunctive of *esse*

Oratio Recta.	*Oratio Obliqua.*
Imperfect	Imperfect Subjunctive
Pluperfect	Pluperfect Subjunctive[1]

γ.

When the Principal Sentence contains a *Command*, the Imperative is, in Oratio Obliqua, replaced by the imperfect —sometimes † present—Subjunctive.

This does not apply to the hortatory Subjunctive which does duty for the first person plural of the Imperative. In this case the change of the Subjunctive to the gerund with *esse*, and of the Subject to a dative, is necessary.

δ.

When the Principal Sentence contains a *Wish*, the verb is of course already Subjunctive. In the normal construction the present tense becomes imperfect, and the person is changed to the third. In the 'vivid' usage †, the only change is that of the person.

ε.

When the Principal Sentence is *Hypothetical*, that is to say, is the apodosis of a whole Conditional Sentence, the changes observed in passing into the Oratio Obliqua accord with the following Schema.

---

[1] Many of the alleged exceptions to the rules here given are probably capable of explanation, and only very few remain. For some of these see Roby, *Lat. Gr.* Bk. IV. c. XXIV. There is an exception to (i) in *Bell. Gall.* I. 43.

SCHEMA IV.

HYPOTHESES.

Oratio Recta.			*Oratio Obliqua.*
Present and Imperfect		If the verb be active	Future participle with *fuisse* — sometimes† *esse*
		If the verb be passive	*Futurum fuisse ut* with Imperfect — some-times† *fore ut*, or *futu-rum esse ut*, with Pre-sent—Subjunctive
Pluperfect		If the verb be active	Future participle with *fuisse* — sometimes Perfect Infinitive
		If the verb be passive	*Futurum fuisse ut* with Imperfect Subjunctive

C. PRONOUNS AND ADVERBS.

The chief changes undergone by pronouns[1] and adverbs in the transition from Oratio Recta to Oratio Obliqua are the following.

Ego. Cases of *ego, meus, nos, noster* become cases of *se* or *ipse, suus.* As *se* may be needed to refer to others than the speaker, the speaker should be distinguished, in all cases where ambiguity may arise, by a case of *ipse.*

tu, vos change to cases of *is*, or, for special emphasis, *ille.*
tuus, vester to *ejus eorum, illius illorum.*

----
[1] See *a*, above.

is	changes to	*ille.*
hic	to	*is, ille.*
iste	to	„ „
hic	to	*illic.*
ibi	to	„
huc	to	*eo, illo.*
eo	to	*illo.*
hodie	to	*eo die, illo die.*
heri	to	*pridie, pridie ejus diei.*
cras	to	*postridie, postridie ejus diei.*
nunc	to	*jam, tunc.*
tunc	to	*illo tempore.*

NOTANDA. *x.* The Oratio Obliqua is often used in Latin where English uses the Direct speech.

y. The introductory verb is sometimes, in Latin, omitted, when the context has prepared us for a coming Speech.

z. When a vocative occurs in English Oratio Recta, we must, when translating into Latin Oratio Obliqua, insert a *reporter's parenthesis*—as (hic eum Caesarem appellavit)—or work the epithet, of course in some other case, into the body of the report, as a substitute for the pronoun *is.*

NOTE III.

The Style of Caesar.

'C. Caesar, gravis auctor linguae Latinae.'

Aul. Gell. IV. 16. 8.

The admiration which Caesar, as a master of Latin style, woke in the most competent of all judges, the great writers of the Golden and of the Silver Age, is abundantly attested.

He was trained, like Cicero, in the Greek Schools of Eloquence and Philosophy. Coming home, in his twenty-third year, he boldly accused Cn. Dolabella of misgovernment in Macedonia. As he had to contend against the 'King of the Courts' Q. Hortensius, and, what was more, against the predominant Party in the State, he lost his case as a matter of course: but at once, 'from that date he took a place, beyond all question, among the leading advocates of the day[1],' and 'rivalled the world's greatest orators[2].' His 'style was brilliant, and free from rhetorical artifice: his voice, his action, and even his figure had a remarkable grandeur and nobility[3].' He spoke 'like a great commander[4].' 'Had

---

[1] Suet. *Caes.* 55. Post accusationem Dolabellae haud dubie principibus patronis annumeratus est.

[2] Tac. *Ann.* XIII. 3. Summis oratoribus aemulus.

[3] Cic. *Brut.* 75, 261. Splendidam quandam minimeque veteratoriam rationem dicendi tenēt, voce, motu, forma etiam magnifica et generosa quodammodo.

[4] Fronto *Ep.* p. 123, Nab. Caesari facultatem dicendi video imperatoriam fuisse.

he but had leisure for the forum, he would have been the
only Roman orator to be named against Cicero: so forcible,
keen and intense was he, that one felt he made speeches
with the same spirit with which he made war[1].'   Only a few
abstracts and fragments of his speeches remain: it is a mis-
fortune that an age of orators is represented to us by one
only, even though that one is Cicero.

The 'other qualities of Caesar's eloquence were enhanced
by a wonderful purity of diction, the study of which he had
made peculiarly his own[2].'   Cicero says: 'Caesar speaks
our language with the greatest purity and taste of, I think,
all our orators: his power to do so is not merely a result of
home habit, but has been attained by very abstruse and
delicate studies, which he has pursued with the deepest
enthusiasm and the most minute industry[3].'   These studies
Caesar published in two books, dedicated to Cicero, bearing
the title 'De Analogia.'   They dealt 'with the art of speaking Latin,' and were 'written most faultlessly in the midst of
the greatest distractions[4]'—during a passage, indeed, over

---

[1] Quintil. X. 1, 114.   C. Caesar si foro modo vacasset, non alius ex
nostris contra Ciceronem nominaretur: tanta in eo vis est, id acumen,
ea concitatio, ut illum eodem animo dixisse quo bellavit appareat.

[2] Quintil. X. 1, 114.   Exornat tamen haec omnia mira sermonis,
cujus proprie studiosus fuit, elegantia.

[3] Cic. *Brut.* 72, 252.   De Caesare ita judico...illum omnium fere
oratorum Latine loqui elegantissime, neque id solum domestica consue-
tudine...sed...multis litteris, et iis quidem reconditis et exquisitis,
summoque studio et diligentia est consecutus.

[4] Cic. *Brut.* 72, 253.   Qui etiam in maximis occupationibus ad te
(*Ciceronem*) de ratione Latine loquendi accuratissime scripserit.

the Alps[1]. Fragments only remain of this treatise: but it must have contributed to the general opinion that Caesar, 'more than any of his contemporaries, spoke pure Latin undefiled[2].'

Ancient criticism on the 'Gallic War' in particular was to the same effect. 'The Commentaries were excellent: all rhetorical finery had been stripped from them like a garment: they were nude, straight, graceful as a statue[3].' Hirtius[4], who added the last Book at Caesar's bidding, explains in his introduction how unwilling he was to undertake the task. 'All the world knows how good and faultless the Commentaries are; I know how easily and rapidly they have been thrown off: yet no other writer has produced anything, with whatever labour, to equal their simple perfection.'

It is seen that an especial attribute of Caesar's style, in the opinion of his countrymen, was what they called 'elegantia.' This word, which down to Cato's time had been used, in a bad sense, to denote over-fastidiousness in diet

---

[1] Suet. *Caes.* 56.

[2] Aul. Gell. XIX. 8, 3. Sermonis praeter alios suae aetatis castissimi.

[3] Cic. *Brut.* 75, 262. Etiam commentarios quosdam scripsit rerum suarum valde quidem probandos, nudi enim sunt, recti, venusti, omni ornatu orationis tamquam veste detracta.

[4] Hirtius, *B. G.* VIII. 1. Nihil tam operose ab aliis esse perfectum, quod non horum elegantia commentariorum superetur...caeteri quam bene atque emendate, nos etiam quam facile et celeriter eos perfecerit scimus.

and dress, seems to have passed into the signification of 'correct taste' in general, but especially 'correct taste' in literature. In Caesar's time the word belonged to fashionable language, and therefore its meanings and uses are often vague and undefined, and far from being able to be expressed in any one word of ours.

But we may inquire what 'elegantia' meant in application to Caesar's speeches and writings. Cicero, who was fond of speaking of oratory as a human figure or as a statue, and of describing oratorical ornament in terms borrowed from the toilet, wrote that about the Commentaries of Caesar there was nothing of 'the curling-irons of rhetoric[1].' By this he wished to say they contained no tags, tropes, figures, antitheses, subtle arrangements of words, catchphrases, sentiments, reflections, elaborate metaphors; in a word, no straining after effect.

But we can also gather positive applications of the term. 'Elegantia' meant the choice of pure Latin words, and their employment in their established significations: Caesar himself laid down the rule that 'an unfamiliar word should be avoided like a rock[2].' It meant precision in the use of the cases, which is so marked in the Commentaries: cases are there applied only in their well-defined and

[1] *Brut.* 75, 262. Calamistri dicendi.

[2] Aul. Gell. I. 10, 4. Id quod a Gaio Caesare, excellentis ingenii ac prudentiae viro, in primo de Analogia libro scriptum est, habe semper in memoria atque in pectore, ut 'tamquam scopulum, sic fugias inauditum atque insolens verbum.'

accepted forces, and are never worked too hard without
the help of prepositions. It meant precision also in the
connection of periods, by means of conjunctions, or the
relative or demonstrative pronouns. The same accuracy
was required in binding together the different clauses of
one period: we often, for instance, have an antecedent
noun repeated in a subsequent relative or demonstrative
predication—to make certainty more certain. Sometimes
the periods may be long; yet analysis will show them to
consist only of plain statements, combined with participial
constructions, or relative, temporal, final and adversative
clauses introduced by the simplest conjunctions or particles.
Caesar's meaning, in his longest periods, is always exact and
clear, except where the text is corrupt.

But words and their grammatical arrangement are not
enough to create Style. This depends still more on good
order, method and symmetry in the distribution of the
subject-matter. Compare Horace, *A. P.* 42 sqq.

> 'Ordinis haec virtus erit et venus, aut ego fallor,
> Ut jam nunc dicat jam nunc debentia dici' &c.

Of this 'lucidus ordo' no better example can be found
than the Commentaries. Style also requires descriptive
power, which comes from keen observation and wise dis-
crimination of important and unimportant details; and,
when the subject rises, Style calls also for the undefinable
magic of eloquence. All this is found in Caesar.

But it is in his minor qualities, his 'elegantia,' his 'sermo castissimus ', that he is so valuable a leader and example to the student of Latinity. His sphere is limited : other great authors must be studied by all who wish to know something of the wide field of Latin Prose. But we may get the best help from him in many great matters—how to write about policies and plans, camps, bridge-making, boat-building, marches and voyages in fair weather and foul ; new scenes, peoples, and customs ; interviews, speeches, negotiations ; battles by land or sea, manoeuvres, tactics, victories, and the settlement of conquered provinces. And it must not be forgotten, if we would have a just reverence for his writings, that, while he was making the historical style, he was also making history.

TABLE OF EXERCISES.

On Caesar *Bell. Gall.*

EXERCISES.

I.

All the materials for this piece will be found in Caes. Bell. Gall., Bk. I., cc. 1—10, *which read carefully, noticing every word and phrase, every construction, and also the order of the words employed by Caesar.*

When we had made every preparation for our departure, we hastened to·Latinitas by forced marches; and, on the appointed day, we reached the borders of that province, over which we expected that we should easily gain complete supremacy, owing to our superiority in intellect. Here we were met by our leader Logus, who pointed out to us the river Syntaxis, across which, he said, lay our quickest route. This river, beginning at Mount Sermo, runs in a north-westerly direction, until it flows into Lake Stylus: it is five miles wide and fifty feet deep. All the bridges had been cut by command of the enemy, and garrisons had been posted at the few places where the stream is fordable. In the regions towards the east and on our rear the heights had been seized by the Inflectiones and Modi, who are not only warlike but always athirst for war; and we were informed that they meant to dispute our way through the passes.

II.

All the materials for this piece will be found in Caes. Bell. Gall., Bk. I., cc. 1—10, *which read carefully, noticing every word and phrase, every construction, and also the order of the words employed by Caesar.*

With these nations we had already established peace, and, as they seemed well-disposed to us, we thought they would abstain from fraud or outrage. But, after the suicide of the old King, Canna, there was no lack of suspicion that he had been murdered; and his wife, Concordia, found herself unable to assert her rights or maintain her supremacy. She had given her daughter in marriage to Norma, the prince of a neighbouring and most powerful people, to whom she sent to ask for aid. The wealthy Anacoluthon, who was desirous of revolution, and popular with the Commons, whose temper he had weakened by his largesses, in the lust of power formed a conspiracy with the young nobles. He had many of these in his debt, or bound to him by kindness. Hence they readily pledged him their word and honour to face every danger and win him the kingdom. Pressed by his influence, the magistrates obliged the queen to appear to defend herself in fetters: the penalty, if she were found guilty, was to be death by fire.

III.

All the materials for this piece will be found in Caes. Bell. Gall., Bk. I., cc. 1—10, which read carefully, noticing every word and phrase, every construction, and also the order of the words employed by Caesar.

On the other hand her son-in-law sent back word that he was ready for action. [1]He had united the Logici to himself as allies, and would be present on the day of trial. He intended, if any harm were done her, to enroll his legions, pass the enemy under the yoke, and burn every town, village and house from the river to the ocean—even if it were a two years' task.

The territory of the Logici has been divided into two parts. The hither portion touches our province. The further portion stretches towards the Physici, who are very bold owing to their wide removal from refined culture, and towards the Metaphysici. The region of the latter looks to the Pole, and is bounded on one side by the Dirae, on the other by the deep sea. All the Metaphysici differ from one another in speech, methods and laws. We learned from the merchants who resort to them, very few in number owing to the character of the district, that there are only two roads, by which sometimes by day, oftener by night, they leave home to carry war into the fields of their neighbours.

- [1] Use *Oratio Obliqua.*

IV.

All the materials for this piece will be found in Caes. Bell. Gall., Bk. I., cc. 1—10, which read carefully, noticing every word and phrase, every construction, and also the order of the words employed by Caesar.

When this affair was made known to us by means of informers, we were deeply grieved, for all hope of homeward return seemed lost. Unwilling, however, to cease our attempt, we took time for thought. First, we appointed an officer to conduct the fortification of our camp, and surrounded it with a wall and a ditch, beyond which we intended to wander little. Then we bought up the crops from the neighbouring districts, as they were particularly fruitful in corn, until we had accumulated ground provisions for six months. We also took care to have ready an abundant supply of draught cattle and waggons. Lastly, we made preparations for constructing a bridge of boats. Our work at length done, on the first of May, we captured, in a cavalry engagement, a man who had great influence both among his own people and among neighbouring communities.

V.

All the materials for this piece will be found in Caes. Bell. Gall., Bk. I., cc. 1—10, which read carefully, noticing every word and phrase, every construction, and also the order of the words employed by Caesar.

As he was a very rich man, of the highest rank, and as we bore in mind that in our fathers' time he had been of no unfriendly temper towards us, we asked him if he thought it possible either to persuade or compel our lately pacified opponents to let us pass. He replied that he thought both things were very easy to be done: but that the former plan was much better, and more free from impediments. He added that no interval should be suffered to elapse, and that the troops should be ready to move from the quarters in which we had wintered, and to cross the hills, while the depth of the streams was at its lowest. We therefore resolved to send him to the forts of the enemy, that by his intercession we might obtain permission to continue our advance through their territory, there being no other route. He readily undertook the commission. The answer came: [1]'If you can force a path through a serried array of troops, you may pass.'

[1] Use *Oratio Obliqua.*

VI.

All the materials for this piece will be found in Caes. Bell. Gall., Bk. I., cc. 10—18, which read carefully, noticing every word and phrase, every construction, and also the order of the words employed by Caesar.

Though we bore this new insult ill, we thought it enough for the present to return the following reply : [1]'We were astonished at the insolence of their boast : our whole conduct towards them had been such as should have deterred their chief magistrate from words so unconscionable. Had they suddenly put away the recollection of their ancient discomfiture and the destruction of their army? If they persisted in wrongdoing, they would have to make us amends. The longer the impunity allowed them by the wisdom of Heaven, the heavier would be their reverse when it came. Let them remember that we had harassed them neither by engagements nor by devastation, neither by plundering nor by foraging; and that we only demanded what they had publicly promised, and ought to have performed.' To this the chief of our embassy added some other arguments privately; but, finding himself put off from day to day, he departed.

[1] Use *Oratio Obliqua.*

VII.

All the materials for this piece will be found in Caes. Bell. Gall., Bk. I., cc. 10—18, which read carefully, noticing every word and phrase, every construction, and also the order of the words employed by Caesar.

On the 21st June, some of the enemy, who had estates on our side of the river, were struck with panic and took refuge with us. They stated that their leader, wishing to avenge both public and private wrongs, had spent his own fortunes, and those of his friends, in collecting large numbers of infantry and cavalry. [1]Two days ago he had measured out the last corn to his army, and, as the other crops were late, had really nothing left but the bare ground. He had assumed the power of life and death, and had so violated traditionary laws and institutions, that he was deserted by many of his countrymen, who had taken to flight and had concealed themselves in the neighbouring woods and cantons. They informed us, further, that he designed to make, in small boats, a night-passage over the river, whose current at this time of the year was remarkably gentle; and that he greatly hoped, by attacking us unawares at the third watch, to inflict some signal disaster.

[1] Use *Oratio Obliqua.*

VIII.

*All the materials for this piece will be found in Caes.
Bell. Gall., Bk. I., cc.* 15—23, *which read carefully, noticing
every word and phrase, every construction, and also the order
of the words employed by Caesar.*

On this we held a council of our officers, and resolved
to send cavalry in advance, to ascertain the movements of
the enemy both by day and night, and also, unless it should
be necessary to turn aside their course for that purpose, to
collect and carry a sufficiently large supply of fodder. At
dawn the next day, while we were holding an assembly,
there rode up to the camp, at full speed, an old man, who,
with many tears and entreaties, begged of us a private
hearing, and said that he could speak more fully in the
absence of the ordinary interpreters. [1] If his request were
denied, he feared, not only his own destruction, but lest
harm should happen to a very large and opulent kingdom.
Our leader, thinking that there must be good cause for
grief so great, consoled him as best he could, then quickly
dismissed the council, and, taking him apart, urged him to
declare boldly and without fear of offence what he desired.

[1] Use *Oratio Obliqua.*

IX.

All the materials for this piece will be found in Caes. Bell. Gall., Bk. I., cc. 17—23, which read carefully, noticing every word and phrase, every construction, and also the order of the words employed by Caesar.

The old man grasped the hand of Logus, and spoke to the following effect. [1] His own name was Usus; for many years he had been king of Loquendum, and had always been warmly disposed to our new empire. One obstacle alone existed; he feared that the distinction of his ancient office was greatly impaired by the revolutionary tendencies of his son Attractus, whom he could no longer restrain. This young man had greatly increased his estate, and now possessed large monetary resources, which we knew were the sinews of war. His generosity had made him very popular, because he had bought up over the heads of the bidders, and then abolished, all dues and taxes; and he had begun, against his father's commands, to maintain at his own expense, and keep about him, large bodies of troops. He had also, without his consent, bestowed his sisters in marriage on the most distinguished of the neighbouring potentates, and by these connections had acquired great influence abroad.

[1] Use *Oratio Obliqua.*

X.

All the materials for this piece will be found in Caes. Bell. Gall., Bk. I., cc. 17—23, which read carefully, noticing every word and phrase, every construction, and also the order of the words employed by Caesar.

[1]He felt that he himself was aimed at in all these proceedings, and he feared he should never be restored to his old influence: that would be sufficient reason for his taking steps in person, yet he himself was prevented from punishing his son by his paternal feelings, as well as by public opinion. But he had long been apprehensive, and his suspicions had been confirmed during the night by a certain circumstance, that the prince intended to use his strength and resources to the injury, or even destruction, of Latinitas. No one could be more sorry for this than he was. He therefore asked our leader to determine what was to be done. He begged him, however, to abstain from over-severe measures, lest the minds of his own subjects should be estranged; for they would think that everything which might take place had been done with his consent. He added that he was acquainted with the honour and moderation of Logus, and did not despair of gaining his request.

[1] Use *Oratio Obliqua.*

XI.

All the materials for this piece will be found in Caes. Bell. Gall., Bk. I., cc. 17—23, *which read carefully, noticing every word and phrase, every construction, and also the order of the words employed by Caesar.*

On hearing the case Logus made inquiry singly of some captives, whom we had taken in a cavalry engagement a few days before, and in the course of cross-examination discovered that part of the king's story was true, part false. He therefore summoned him to his presence, warned him of what he had heard, pointed out the risk he had run, urged him to avoid for the future everything that might lead to suspicion, and set a guard over him to watch his actions.

The king entreated, at greater length than before, that no over-severe wound should be inflicted by Logus upon his son. Logus, on his part, did not wish to hurt the father's mind by any heavy punishment, and had great hopes of maintaining the kingdom, thinking that the rest of the nation would be alarmed by the king's flight. Still he resolved that the young prince must be restrained before he could make any attempt. He therefore imparted his designs to Ordo, an officer distinguished for military skill, in whom he reposed perfect confidence.

XII.

All the materials for this piece will be found in Caes| Bell. Gall., Bk. I., cc. 17—23, which read carefully, noticing every word and phrase, every construction, and also the order of the words employed by Caesar.

This officer started with one legion, and after he had advanced about ten miles from the camp, learned from the scouts that the prince had taken up his position on a hill seven miles away. They reported that the ascent to the summit was easy, if a sudden attack were made from all sides at once. Ordo at first drew up his troops in order of battle, and began to lead them to the foot of the hill. But as he had received strict orders from Logus to avoid an engagement unless his forces were discovered by the enemy, he changed his design; and, apprised by fugitives that the prince had only provisions remaining for two days, he re- solved to cut off his supplies. Bending his march round the hill, he waited till the prince should be obliged to strike his camp, intending then to harass the rear of his column, and, following him at a moderate distance, to drive him in the direction of our camp.

XIII.

All the materials for this piece will be found in Caes. Bell. Gall., Bk. I., cc. 22—29, which read carefully, noticing every word and phrase, every construction, and also the order of the words employed by Caesar.

Meanwhile Logus had been informed of what was going on, and led the regiments from the camp in order to attack the nearest side of the hill. He had also sent instructions to Ordo to make an assault, simultaneously with himself, at the fourth watch. In this way our troops surrounded the mountain, and began to ascend, in two divisions, at the appointed hour. The enemy on the ridge, however, had perceived our movement, detecting us by our arms and standards, and prepared to resist our coming. In dense array, and hurling their pikes from above, they wounded many of our soldiers, and frequently broke our line, thus checking our onset. For a long time the engagement continued without decisive result. At last Ordo, drawing his sword, cheered on his men, and, advancing in phalanx on the exposed flank of the enemy, forced them to give ground.

XIV.

All the materials for this piece will be found in Caes. Bell. Gall., Bk. I., cc. 22—29, which read carefully, noticing every word and phrase, every construction, and also the order of the words employed by Caesar.

Even yet he could not break their line, for not a man of them was seen to look behind him. When their shields were pierced or riveted together by a lance-thrust, thus laying them at a great disadvantage, they would shake their left arms free from their defences and fight with unprotected person. Worn out by wounds, they at length retired to the spot where they had collected their baggage, and formed a laager. Even then they thrust their assegais between the wheels, and resisted with such remarkable valour, that our troops had still failed to become masters of their camp when night came on.

In this way the battle had raged from dawn till evening without intermission. During the whole of the night, however, deserters poured in, either driven by utter destitution, for they had nothing to stay hunger with, or in fear of being tortured if taken in arms. These, throwing themselves at our feet, begged for quarter, with tears.

XV.

*All the materials for this piece will be found in Caes.
Bell. Gall., Bk. I., cc. 23—29, which read carefully, noticing
every word and phrase, every construction, and also the order
of the words employed by Caesar.*

When Logus found this out, he sent messengers to offer
peace. "'He would receive on terms of surrender, and
provide with food, all who would come over to him. It was
vain for them to try to renew the fight; and flight could not
be concealed, as they were hemmed in. One hope of safety
they had; let them send hostages and yield up their arms.
If Attractus would dismiss his Greek auxiliaries and consent
to make his apologies, he should have the same legal rights
and equal liberty with his father. All who still delayed he
would treat as belligerents.' His special purpose in making
this offer, was to prevent the desolation of a district remarkable for the excellence of its products. Won by these conditions, they obeyed. The total number of those who
capitulated was, after a census, found to be 1,500. A list of
all who were capable of bearing arms was entered in a table.
The vanquished returned home; we remained for three days
to bury the slain, and, after the lapse of that interval, were
led back to camp.

¹ Use *Oratio Obliqua.*

XVI.

*All the materials for this piece will be found in Caes.
Bell. Gall., Bk. I., cc. 29—36, which read carefully, noticing
every word and phrase, every construction, and also the order
of the words employed by Caesar.*

By the battle fought at the Hill the war was ended : we
had once and for ever crushed the forces of the enemy. The
rule of war is, indeed, that the victor may do as he will with
the vanquished ; and we might have picked out the richest
portion of their territory for our own habitation. We,
however, took no such airs to ourselves, thinking that we had
obtained sufficient satisfaction from the communities for their
wrongdoings. It was decided to make them tributary, and
bind them by oath to remain for ever under our suzerainty.
A deputation of leading men came to beg us to proclaim a
general assembly on an appointed day. We replied that
the request could not be granted, as a multitude could not
be gathered at any one suitable spot without great difficulty
of transport. This being made known, a deputy, represent-
ing the national feeling, thanked us for treating them so
kindly. [1]They had expected that we should exact the most
severe punishment, and that they would have to face the
worst agonies. They would abide by the conditions fixed
for them, and there should be, between his countrymen and
ours, eternal amity. His speech ended, the assembly dis-
persed.

[1] Use *Oratio Obliqua.*

XVII.

All the materials for this piece will be found in Caes. Bell. Gall., Bk. I., cc. 29—36, which read carefully, noticing every word and phrase, every construction, and also the order of the words employed by Caesar.

We had great hopes that our kinsmen, whom we had left behind in the happiest circumstances, would come as early as possible to congratulate us on our new victory. No one met us : all had forsaken their homes, and crossed to a neutral region. Wondering what could be the cause of this, we went to ask them personally what business they had there. All were seated on the ground, as if broken by disaster, with dismal, downcast looks. We spoke to them encouragingly, and promised again and again to look after them : but, though we strove and struggled to get a reply, we could not extract a sound. They remained lost in a dumb melancholy. However, so vigorously did we promise that whoever chose should speak without danger of mischief to himself, and pledged ourselves that none should reveal what might be entrusted to us, that at length one youth fell weeping at our feet, and begged to be heard in the closest privacy.

XVIII.

*All the materials for this piece will be found in Caes.
Bell. Gall., Bk. I., cc. 29—36, which read carefully, noticing
every word and phrase, every construction, and also the order
of the words employed by Caesar.*

[1] He spoke for his own life and that of his friends, whom
we must not think to have taken offence when we invited
them to reply : he spoke for all, praying it might be for the
good of the commonwealth. They had declined to unite
with us, when we carried war into Latinitas, simply because
they wished to do nothing which the rest did. This had
turned out less to their advantage than to ours, or rather had
been the worse for them. First, we knew that the holder
of chief authority was Cultus, and that, as they were in his
power, he would, were anything betrayed, exemplify tortures
of every kind. Secondly, two new factions had arisen: a
Gaul had been brought over, a wrathful and impetuous man,
at whose nod and beck everything was to take place, and
also a German, whose mode of life was not incomparable
with the arrogance of the other. These men haughtily bade
them work : such tyrannies were intolerable and no longer
to be endured.

[1] Use *Oratio Obliqua.*

XIX.

All the materials for this piece will be found in Caes. Bell. Gall., Bk. I., cc. 29—36, which read carefully, noticing every word and phrase, every construction, and also the order of the words employed by Caesar.

[1] Against this they (the speaker and his friends) had struggled more than once, but had been defeated and had suffered great calamity. They had had no chance of flight; and each would have to pledge himself to be obedient, as his relations, who yearly paid dues for his benefit, refused relief. Neither the German nor the Gaul, both veterans in arms, refrained from acting as he thought proper, more especially as Cultus, when appealed to for help, declared that neither should be hampered in the exercise of his authority. Unless we could lend some assistance, the result, in a few years, would be that everybody would be forced to learn the German and Gallic tongues. This danger they were now making a great effort to meet and defy, and, for their own part, were ready to try their fortune.

[1] Use *Oratio Obliqua.*

XX.

All the materials for this piece will be found in Caes. Bell. Gall., Bk. I., cc. 36—41, *which read carefully, noticing every word and phrase, every construction, and also the order of the words employed by Caesar.*

He added that, after inquiry among travelling merchants and among his friends, he had been informed that the Gauls and the Germans were giants, of inconceivable cruelty, and that no one could bear even the flash of their eyes. Here he was unable to restrain his tears, and begged that, with our permission, he might be allowed to depart.

When all this was reported, a sudden panic demoralized, in no ordinary degree, the whole army. It began with some civilians, who, though they had not any military experience, had accompanied us out of friendship. By degrees, however, throughout the camp, old campaigners, men and officers, were unable to keep their faces, and, each alleging special urgent reasons for retiring, hid themselves in their tents, to sign their wills or bewail their doom.

XXI.

All the materials for this piece will be found in Caes. Bell. Gall., Bk. I., cc. 36—41, which read carefully, noticing every word and phrase, every construction, and also the order of the words employed by Caesar.

On perceiving this, all who kept their posts, through feelings of honour, or because they little cared to give themselves out as cowards, while compassionating the general danger of their friends, were deeply angered ; and, fearing mutiny, hastened to call, as quickly as possible, a council which officers of every grade were summoned to attend. We thought we must take very great precautions lest a new force join the foe, and that with all our own troops we should occupy some naturally fortified position. Not three days' journey distant there was a mountain, of such height that provisions could be conveniently carried up : a river, circling its base—and, where the river fails, narrow gorges, marshes, and great forests,—made a complete citadel, which offered great facilities for resistance, and contained plenty of everything serviceable for defence. We resolved to strike camp, about the fourth watch, the next night, and advance thither by forced marches, night and day.

XXII.

All the materials for this piece will be found in Caes. Bell. Gall., Bk. I., cc. 36—41, which read carefully, noticing every word and phrase, every construction, and also the order of the words employed by Caesar.

We then investigated our route, by means of scouts, and learned that it required a circuit of not more than forty-nine miles, through regions free from difficulty. Each of our senior captains was most ready to conduct the war, and not one hesitated to undertake the duties of commander with a light heart. Whilst we had formed an excellent opinion of all, especially the military tribunes and the officers in charge of the cavalry, we still thought that they were too inexperienced, and that they wished to realise at once what they should destine to a future day. Fearing, then, that they might blunder or be unlucky, and knowing that success is won more by skill and judgment than by bravery, we offered to Logus, in whom we had particular confidence, and of whose indefatigability it was impossible to lose hope, the whole conduct of the campaign. Learning our request, although he stood unarmed, with armed men on both sides of him, he seemed to be wholly unmoved by that fact, and administered to us a violent rebuke.

XXIII.

All the materials for this piece will be found in Caes. Bell. Gall., Bk. I., cc. 36—41, which read carefully, noticing every word and phrase, every construction, and also the order of the words employed by Caesar.

[1]'Are you barbarians? Is this a rising of slaves? Has some crime of yours been detected? Are you not wearied by the length of the last war? If frenzy drives you wantonly to leave your duty, at any rate decide by what plans you are to be led. All your lives long, your good fortune has been remarkable. Cultus has always most anxiously desired your affection. You have tried him, and can judge how much kindness resides in him. He has indulged you and put the fullest trust in your manliness. Will you reject his favour? Here is an occasion for your courage. He always gives free access to himself. Show what your experience and training have done for you, and decide whether honour and duty or panic shall prevail. Meet him, offer him amends, and your apology will be accepted.'

The fairness of this proposal being felt, a remarkable change took place in our minds and tempers, and an active desire to do our duty was suddenly created within us.

[1] Use *Oratio Obliqua.*

XXIV.

All the materials for this piece will be found in Caes. Bell. Gall., Bk. I., cc. 41—47, which read carefully, noticing every word and phrase, every construction, and also the order of the words employed by Caesar.

But, after the news had been carried out to the general body of our kinsmen, that we did not repudiate these terms, and that we were willing to trust our lives to a conference, they complained at length, in terms not at all complimentary. After saying a good deal about their own excellencies, they declared that they were not so wanting in knowledge of the world as to be unaware that our friendship was feigned. [1]They were bound to suspect that we wished, by with-drawing on terms of surrender, to gratify the commander-in-chief, lose nothing of our own, obtain rewards, and rise in favour and position. They were afraid they were treacher-ously entrapped: we had not come of our own accord, but had been summoned and sent by the enemy for the purpose of spying out and destroying them. They had thought we should have been, not their ruin, but a loyal support to them, if active measures had to be taken. If we would not help, at least let us retire, and leave them free possession of the spot.

[1] Use *Oratio Obliqua.*

XXV.

All the materials for this piece will be found in Caes. Bell. Gall., Bk. I., cc. 41—47, which read carefully, noticing every word and phrase, every construction, and also the order of the words employed by Caesar.

Here they opened fire on us. Logus would not allow us to return a single shot. So we replied in words, that as far as we were concerned, they might abolish the old ties which existed between us; but we entreated them not to obstruct us in the exercise of our rights; and we said much to show reason why they should not persevere in their undertaking.

Amid these contentions it was ascertained, by means of messages, that Cultus was approaching; and a foot-soldier of the legion slyly remarked that he would give a big bounty if any one would at once get him enlisted in the Horse. On learning the General's arrival, we began to be sanguine that our friends would come back to their senses and cease their obstinate behaviour. At length Cultus was seen to ride towards us along the plain and to station his troops near a fairly large earth-mound, about half-way between the two legions. After deputies had passed to and fro, a time was fixed for the colloquy.

XXVI.

All the materials for this piece will be found in Caes. Bell. Gall., Bk. I., cc. 41—47, *which read carefully, noticing every word and phrase, every construction, and also the order of the words employed by Caesar.*

When we arrived, Cultus began his speech by asking us to look on him as a friend, not as a foe. [1]The favours he had bestowed on us were a proof of this. He did not wish to recapitulate his generosity; but we had no fair reason for asking more. Just as he sought our friendship, so we should not reject his. In bringing over the German and the Gaul, he was not really attacking our liberty. Both were men of the highest worth and the greatest courtesy, had been presented with our own civil privileges, and, on account of their long familiarity with our language, were highly fitted for the command. His habits did not permit him to desert such worthy allies. They would be an ornament to the army, and would carry out any advisable wars without hazard to the selected legion. When he had spoken more largely on the good qualities of his legates, he left, according to his fixed custom, to attend the Congresses; and this broke up the colloquy.

[1] Use *Oratio Obliqua.*

XXVII.

All the materials for this piece will be found in Caes. Bell. Gall., Bk. I., cc. 46—54, which read carefully, noticing every word and phrase, every construction, and also the order of the words employed by Caesar.

Then, if never before, the fighting spirit fell on the whole army, which refused to be confined within walled camps ; and certainly, if any one wished to be under arms and see service, opportunity was not wanting under the new commanders. We engaged in almost daily battles ; and it was our custom each to select one man, from the force at large, under whose eyes we fought, and so had each a witness of our gallantry. Our order of battle was alway threefold : the first and second lines were held by the cavalry, 8,000 in number, because they could advance further and retire more rapidly than infantry : the third by as many legionaries in phalanx. The light-armed auxiliaries we used on the flanks, nation by nation, to make a display. So we advanced our camp speedily along the hither and the further bank of the Rhine, until the season required us to return home. After finishing two great wars in one summer, we were led back to our winter quarters.

XXVIII.

All the materials for this piece will be found in Caes. Bell. Gall., Bk. I., cc. 46—54, which read carefully, noticing every word and phrase, every construction, and also the order of the words employed by Caesar.

On our arrival at the larger camp, a circumstance occurred which gave us quite as much pleasure as our victory. A dear friend, whom we had lost by a disaster which not even our good fortune could lighten, was restored to us, safe and sound, after a marvellous escape from the hands of the enemy. Amid our joyful congratulations he told us the manner of his flight. 'The savages,' said he, 'cut us off from relief by their numbers, and so violently crushed our lines that we had not room to use our lances. Dropping them, we fought with the sabre, hand to hand. The sweep of our swords the enemy met by hurling upon them the bodies of the dead: many too were found to leap on the shields of their friends, and so deal blows from above.

XXIX.

All the materials for this piece will be found in Caes. Bell. Gall., Bk. I., cc. 46—54, which read carefully, noticing every word and phrase, every construction, and also the order of the words employed by Caesar.

The captain in command of the cavalry showed himself both strong and quick: wherever the business was particularly rough, he charged to the assistance of our hard-pressed comrades, and revived the fight. At length, having received a serious wound, he fell from his horse, and was immediately surrounded and despatched by the foe. So the fight ran sharp and long, heavy blows being given and taken on both sides, and we keep the enemy at bay till evening. At sunset, however, they received auxiliaries, and their multitude finished the work, and broke our squares. Fight became flight; yet very few turned their backs. Only three of us were taken prisoners: the rest the foe followed up and slaughtered. We were dragged by guards to a camp, surrounded by waggons,—situated about three miles beyond the scene of the battle,—and there flung into chains.

XXX.

All the materials for this piece will be found in Caes. Bell. Gall., Bk. I., cc. 46—54, which read carefully, noticing every word and phrase, every construction, and also the order of the words employed by Caesar.

Lots were immediately drawn to decide whether we should be roasted to death at once or not. By luck's favour, and also because the women, with out-spread hands and wild prophecies, demonstrated that it was not lawful to kill a captive before the new moon, we were kept for another time. Little hope of flight remained. None the less, next morning we wrenched off our fetters, ran forward and caught a horse. One mounted : the other two, thanks to speed won by old practice, were able, holding on by the mane, to keep pace for many consecutive hours. About noon we reached a river, which at first we intended to swim across, trusting our strength. However we got hold of a small boat that was tied to the bank, and, setting adrift some other craft which were there, that the enemy, if they had the wish, might not have the ability to make chase, we found our deliverance.'

XXXI.

All the materials for this piece will be found in Caes. Bell. Gall., Bk. II., cc. 1—13, which read carefully, noticing every word and phrase, every construction, and also the order of the words employed by Caesar.

After the King Historicus had brought back his brothers and kinsmen, and all who were connected with them by blood or marriage, to the broad and fertile plains from which, as we have shown before, they had in ancient times been expelled, he continued to maintain supreme authority, and, by the unanimous consent of his people, all offices of state were, on account of his justice and practical wisdom, laid upon him alone. Frequent tidings reached the neighbouring communities also, and created among them a remarkable opinion of his excellent qualities, in the reports of which all informants invariably agreed. These peoples therefore no longer took it ill that an alien multitude were settling and making themselves at home upon their borders. They felt how much it concerned their national interests that a region, which in their fathers' recollection and their own had always been harassed,—partly by frivolous revolutionaries, partly by those who, having means to hire supporters, everywhere established themselves in petty kingships,—should now at length be tranquillised, and allow them in security to enjoy the richness of their own lands.

XXXII.

All the materials for this piece will be found in Caes. Bell. Gall., Bk. II., cc. 1—13, *which read carefully, noticing every word and phrase, every construction, and also the order of the words employed by Caesar.*

At the beginning of summer, therefore, they sent a deputation of their leading men, offering to put themselves and all they had under the King's protection. [1]This had been decided on in the general council of all the communities which are collectively called Logographi, and live under the same laws and the same government. [1]A special reason, besides other motives, had led them to this resolution : owing to the extent of their territory they could not easily gather for self-defence, if foes attacked them on all sides at once. The King graciously received their submission, at the same time instructing them to garrison the bridge on the river (which was situated at the further limits of their province), to allow no body of troops to cross or enter their boundaries, to fortify their towns, and also to bring to him, as hostages, a certain number of those who were of highest birth and prestige among them. He undertook, himself, to keep their rear safe from any foe. With these instructions, having complimented them handsomely in his speech, he dismissed the deputies; who, having thus gained their request, and having promised to perform his commands punctually and punctiliously, departed to their several homes.

[1] Use *Oratio Obliqua.*

XXXIII.

All the materials for this piece will be found in Caes. Bell. Gall., Bk. II., cc. 1—13, which read carefully, noticing every word and phrase, every construction, and also the order of the words employed by Caesar.

Suddenly there came news. [1]The Mythologi, who were said to compose the third part of the Logographi, were in arms. The causes of this conspiracy were two. In the first place, they feared that an army of Historicus might winter with them and consume their home supply of provisions. In the second place, they were egged on by a certain prince, eminent among all who dwelt on this side of the river for his courage and his following. This prince, by name Heliomantis, found himself less able to attain his ambitious aims under the King's suzerainty: hence it came that he urged his neighbours to offer an armed resistance. He promised 5,000 picked men himself, demanded supreme control of the war, and put on great military airs. Corps were collecting, an army was concentrating, with unknown rapidity. The people could not be frightened from sympathising with him, or even persuaded to delay a little while. The rising was like a flight—each man anxious to be first on the road. As was shown by fires and smoke the previous night, they had burnt their hamlets and houses; and they had taken themselves and all their chattels to their chief city, Nephelococcygia.

[1] Use *Oratio Obliqua* to the end of this piece.

XXXIV.

All the materials for this piece will be found in Caes. Bell. Gall., Bk. II., cc. 1—13, which read carefully, noticing every word and phrase, every construction, and also the order of the words employed by Caesar.

The King was deeply angered at these tidings, the more so, since the facts were confirmed by his spies, and also by a despatch from an officer, whom he had commissioned to watch proceedings and keep him well-informed. This officer wrote that he had not yet completed his investigations, and did not know what forces each community had promised to contribute. [1] He thought, however, that altogether they would be able to make up a total of 45,000 armed men, and that the light auxiliaries, who were drawn from the most remote districts and were reckoned very formidable warriors, would be about as many more. The town was situated in a position naturally advantageous for defence. The slight eminence, on which it lay, had on each side sharp declivities, and where, in front, it merged with a gentle slope into the plain, there was a marsh of considerable magnitude. But the King would be able to dispense with storming operations: the fury of the townsmen was such that they would be sure to sally forth to attack him. His troops need only wait under arms till they began the passage over the marsh, and might then take them, on such unfavourable ground, at a great disadvantage.

[1] Use *Oratio Obliqua* to the end of this piece.

XXXV.

*All the materials for this piece will be found in Caes.
Bell. Gall., Bk. II. cc. 1—13, which read carefully, noticing
every word and phrase, every construction, and also the order
of the words employed by Caesar.*

He at once resolved that he must not hesitate to lead an
army to the town, for the purpose of keeping the contingents
of the enemy apart,—lest he should have to join issue
simultaneously with multitudes so vast,—and also for the
purpose of testing their military prowess. He hastened to
send scouts in advance, fearing ambuscade ; then,—having,
on the route, left two newly enrolled legions in redoubts, to
secure the safe conduct of his supplies, and to act as supports
if occasion should anywhere arise,—after a forced march,
about sunset, he drew near the hill, and pitched his camp a
mile and a half from the city.   During the remnant of day-
light he fortified the camp all round with cross trenches,
19 feet deep and 500 yards long, and, at the end of each,
erected towers, in which he planted artillery, lest the enemy
—as, from their numbers, they easily could do—should
surround him and take his troops on the flank during an
engagement.   This done, and a mound thrown up on the
inner side, he collected a supply of fodder, and then began
to prepare the necessary engines for storming a city.

XXXVI.

All the materials for this piece will be found in Caes. Bell. Gall., Bk. II. cc. 1—13, which read carefully, noticing every word and phrase, every construction, and also the order of the words employed by Caesar.

At the first streak of day a great shouting was heard, and it was discovered that the enemy, noisily and tumultuously, were leaving the city and descending the hill. With great dash, though with disordered ranks, they crossed the marsh. Presently an immense number of archers and slingers poured round the camp, and their heavy fire allowed no standing on the ramparts, which it had soon stripped of their defenders. The soldiers in the towers gallantly, but with difficulty, held out against furious assaults. They were only enabled to do so by the magnitude of the works, which were such as the enemy had never seen or heard of before—though many, indeed, in the boldest manner tried to cross the trenches, which were filled with bodies of the slain. One officer, in command of a tower, sent word that most of his men were cut down, and that with so few defenders he could not hold out much longer, unless assistance were sent up. Meanwhile, however, the enemy's supply of missiles had run short, and, finding they were deceived in their hope of taking the camp by storm, they withdrew. Though ignorant of the cause of their retirement, the King's cavalry at once followed them up, and, falling on their rear, slew great numbers; then, as night closed, returned, according to orders, to camp.

XXXVII.

All the materials for this piece will be found in Caes. Bell. Gall., Bk. II., cc. 1—13, which read carefully, noticing every word and phrase, every construction, and also the order of the words employed by Caesar.

As the cavalry engagement had gone in favour of the King, the legions became filled with a hope of gaining the town and with an enthusiastic desire to make the assault, wishing to show that unmounted troops were no whit inferior to horsemen. The King himself thought it best to follow up the foe, before they could recover from their panic and flight. With this resolution, he struck his camp about midnight, and, using as guides the prisoners of yesterday, found out the fordable places of the marsh, and carried his army across. On reaching the foot of the slope, he drew up his line of battle, and moved upon the gates. Meanwhile mantlets were wheeled up, and, under their shelter, or else under locked shields, the soldiers began to sap the wall. Historicus had expected the engagement to be keen : but the townsmen, who had thought themselves out of danger, startled by his rapidity, and utterly disorganised, gave up all hope of defence and sought refuge in flight. Then, issuing from the gate, the old men and children, holding forth their outspread hands, after their fashion, to show that they were non-combatants, sued for quarter.

XXXVIII.

All the materials for this piece will be found in Caes. Bell. Gall., Bk. II., cc. 14—19, *which read carefully, noticing every word and phrase, every construction, and also the order of the words employed by Caesar.*

As soon as all arms had been collected from the city and given up, one of the surrendered was chosen as spokesman for the rest. [1]'I understand,' he said, 'what a disaster has been inflicted on my country by the authors of the present plot, who have enlarged the influence of Heliomantis (hoping by his help and resources to conduct any war that may befall), and have persuaded the rest of their countrymen to secede from the King, although they wished to remain on terms of loyal friendship with him. We have shared the fortunes of war with our leaders, yet these have fled : we, after their desertion, are left to suffer outrage and indignity, and to be reduced to slavery. It would be no trouble to the King to put us all to death. Still I beg he will exhibit his customary mercy and humanity to those whom age or sex renders incapable of bearing arms. In the old time we were a leading state, our men rude but of great bravery. Of late, wine and other luxuries have been imported by the merchants ; and, under their influence, we have cast away our hereditary courage ; our tempers relax and sink into lethargy.'

[1] Use *Oratio Obliqua.*

XXXIX.

All the materials for this piece will be found in Caes. Bell. Gall., Bk. II., cc. 14—19, which read carefully, noticing every word and phrase, every construction, and also the order of the words employed by Caesar.

The King then made inquiry of some of the captives as to the nature of their troops and the quarter to which they had retired—only a few pickets of cavalry being in sight, and these already far off. He learnt that whatever strength the enemy possessed lay in infantry: [1]reinforcements were however expected, and were certainly on their way. It had been arranged before the battle that, in case of disaster, they should seek concealment on a hill distant about three days' journey. This hill sprang from the river with a regular ascent, and was wooded at the summit. In the woods they lay in hiding. They had made the place not only impassable, but impenetrable to the sight, by cutting and bending bushy young trees, and twisting among them brambles and thorns, so as to form a hedge-like fortification: through this, however, they themselves could continually dart forth, attack, and return, with such inconceivable rapidity, that they seemed to be upon the foe, and back in the woods, almost at the same instant of time.

For this hill the army started. The order of march was not the same as on ordinary occasions. One unencumbered legion led, under orders to advance only as far as the ground was level,—never up hill,—that the large quantity of baggage might not check the march. The baggage intervened between this legion and the rest, which marched under knapsacks: and cavalry closed the column.

[1] Use *Oratio Obliqua* to the end of the paragraph.

XL.

All the materials for this piece will be found in Caes. Bell. Gall., Bk. II., cc. 20—28, *which read carefully, noticing every word and phrase, every construction, and also the order of the words employed by Caesar.*

At evening, while the camp was being fortified on the slope of a hill, the King sent one officer from each of the legions to observe from the ridge any movements of the enemy. They at once reported that they saw, over the thick hedges which obstructed the view from the lower ground, large bodies of the foe, at no great distance, advancing rapidly on both sides. When the King heard this, he saw how things stood, and in what danger those were who had gone far in front of the camp to obtain materials for the rampart; he ordered the recall to be sounded, and sent off the cavalry to bring in the stragglers. The cavalry left nothing to be desired in the speed with which they executed this command, and soon a multitude poured in at the rear-gate of the camp—camp-followers in headlong flight, light-armed infantry, breathless and spent, yet eager to rush to arms. Amid much shouting and din the line of battle was formed—there was no time to put on helmets, or uncase shields. Each man rallied at the first standard which he reached, not to miss the chances of the fight in seeking his proper company. Having given the necessary orders as far as the narrowness of the time allowed, the King called the military tribunes to the front of the line of battle.

XLI.

All the materials for this piece will be found in Caes. Bell. Gall., Bk. II., cc. 20—28, which read carefully, noticing every word and phrase, every construction, and also the order of the words employed by Caesar.

'¹'Owing to the nearness of the foe,' said he, 'I have had everything to do at once, and my line of battle is haphazard rather than scientific. In the engagement you must not wait for orders. One man cannot foresee what must be done in every part of the field. Wherever chance may bring you, you must take the proper measures on your own responsibility. But you have had your training in the battles of the past, and can lay down your duties for yourselves as well as any other man could teach you them.'

He then hastened both to the right and to the left wing, and encouraged the troops with a few words.

'¹'I have no time for a long speech, and I see that your minds are already steeled for combat. Two things relieve our difficulties, your skill and your experience. Keep cool: stand your ground: support one another. Each man do his best, for he will fight under his general's eye. Amid the unfavourableness of our circumstances, remember your glorious past. Conquerors have no difficulties, the conquered nothing but dangers: and heroism renders the hardest things easy.'

¹ Use *Oratio Obliqua.*

XLII.

All the materials for this piece will be found in Caes. Bell. Gall., Bk. II., cc. 20—28, which read carefully, noticing every word and phrase, every construction, and also the order of the words employed by Caesar.

The enemy, who in the mean time had been swarming the hill without intermission, were now within a spear's cast, and, although the uneven nature of the ground was a great disadvantage to them, charged the right wing with the utmost violence and intrepidity. At the same time, on the other side, the signal was given to join battle and move forward. Checkered fortunes ensued. At the first shock the troops on the right wing, being outflanked and hard pressed, began to move higher up the hill, and to fall back on the camp. The standard-bearer was killed, the standard lost; most of the officers had fallen or were wounded. Some of the men even slunk out of the fight, and only tried to dodge the missiles. There was no regularly posted reserve, which could be sent up to the rescue.

The King saw at once that matters were critical. Snatching a sword from the nearest soldier—he had come without his own—he rushed to the front, called on the surviving officers by name, and bade them open their tight-packed lines, to give room for the use of the sword. At his arrival the soldiers were inspired with a hope that they might wipe out their disgrace by gallantry. The fight revived: the advance of the enemy was checked; and by degrees the other legions united and bore down on the foe.

XLIII.

All the materials for this piece will be found in Caes. Bell. Gall. Bk. II., cc. 20—28, *which read carefully, noticing every word and phrase, every construction, and also the order of the words employed by Caesar.*

A great change now took place. The legionaries discharged their pikes, followed up with the sword, forced the enemy down hill, and cut down great numbers of them. Still they fought on in forlorn hope, or in despair, and could not but be esteemed as men of unrivalled valour. As the front ranks fell, those behind them sprang upon the heaped bodies of the slain, and, when their own javelins were lost, caught and returned the pikes that were hurled against them. The unarmed grappled with the armed : even those who lay wounded to the death, upon the ground, propped themselves on their shields and fought afresh. When they were utterly routed, they continued to resist their pursuers to the very end of their flight, battling on the river banks and even in the tidal waters to which they were driven. Their rear, left in charge of their baggage, was surrounded and cut to pieces.

But the King took the utmost care of the women and children, and treated all poor suppliants with compassion : he even allowed them to retain their towns, on condition that they kept out of mischief. The captives, in recounting their disaster, declared that their race had been almost annihilated : out of 45,000, barely 500 survived who were able to bear arms.

XLIV.

All the materials for this piece will be found in Caes. Bell. Gall., Bk. III., cc. 8—16, which read carefully, noticing every word and phrase, every construction, and also the order of the words employed by Caesar.

Meanwhile the sea-faring people, who are revolutionaries to a man and quickly stirred to secession and rebellion, entered suddenly on a new and unexpected policy. The plot began with the Rhapsodi, whose influence is by far the most extensive over all the sea-board, as they had the largest command of ships and were superior to their neighbours in naval science : hence they easily won over the rest to their own views. [1]'Other peoples,' they urged, 'have refused to be tributary or to remain in subordination : we think we may do as much. We fail to understand what crime we have committed : yet when we sent a common deputation to the King, our deputies—an office religiously respected all the world over, whose privileges are upheld even by barbarians— have been detained. Many other wrongs spur us to war. Besides, we are born haters of the lot of the slave, lovers of freedom : let us remain in that freedom which is ours by inheritance. Unite, conspire, win allies, send for helpers : swear together to act wholly in concert and to share one fortune ! We need not despair of our chances, but may trust largely in the natural advantages of our situation. 'Tis labour in vain to try to storm our cities : and, even supposing that we are disappointed in everything, yet no one can check our escape. Pursuit is one thing in a land-locked sea, another thing on the open sweep of infinite ocean.'

[1] Use *Oratio Obliqua.*

XLV.

All the materials for this piece will be found in Caes. Bell. Gall., Bk. III., cc. 8—16, *which read carefully, noticing every word and phrase, every construction, and also the order of the words employed by Caesar.*

Informed of this movement, the King gave orders to gather a large fleet, muster crews, and provide ample supplies of all ship's stores and equipments : then, as soon as the season allowed, he hastened in force to the revolted communities. His voyage was hampered by the fewness of the harbours, and also by the ignorance of the regions shown by the pilots ; he was delayed, too, by stress of weather. At length however he drew near the port at which the enemy had collected every available vessel. As he came in sight, the enemy's fleet sailed out to meet him, perfectly equipped with every engine of war, and carrying on board all their fighting men, as well as all of advanced rank, or of advanced age, in whom any practical wisdom resided. Wherever a near view of the sea was possible, the shores were crowded by their friends, by whom no deed of special gallantry would pass unnoticed. The King distributed his vessels rather widely to leeward, fearing that the enemy, if, as was pretty probable, they were worsted, would, as their chief hope lay in their sails, run before the wind and escape. The engagement was short. The enemy tried some ineffectual ramming : the King's crews grappled and boarded them; or cut their halyards with long boathooks, so that the yards dropped and the ships were wholly helpless. A dead calm also fell, favourable for finishing the business. Recognising the greatness of their peril, the enemy rowed hastily back, and, thanks to the interposition of night, found safety behind their moles and breakwaters.

XLVI.

All the materials for this piece will be found in Cæs. Bell. Gall., Bk. III., cc. 8—16, which read carefully, noticing every word and phrase, every construction, and also the order of the words employed by Caesar.

There were certainly difficulties in concluding the war by storming the towns, owing to their situations. They were placed on the outer verge of forelands or spit-heads. The foot-roads were cut up by creeks, which were impassable when the flood-tide ran in from the sea, as it did every twelve hours, and were dangerous even at the ebb. The King hesitated what plan of attack to adopt. At length he built some vessels of great bulk and strength, with very high bows, but rather flat keels, so that they could settle down and take the ground at the ebb with ease. He also strengthened them with 12-inch beams, fastened together with iron bolts a finger in thickness, so that if the tide was rough and the wind boisterous—the occurrence of both of which accidents he had to fear—they could stand any amount of knocking about. These structures he moved up the creeks, close by the city, by oars and poles, moored them by chain cables, and then, high on the prows, ran up great towers level with the city walls.

This done, the enemy had no means of defence. After several towns had been stormed, they surrendered unconditionally. The King thought it necessary to make an example of them; and therefore put the ringleaders to death, and sold all their counsellors as captive slaves.

XLVII.

All the materials for this piece will be found in Caes. Bell. Gall., Bk. IV., cc. 1—3, *which read carefully, noticing every word and phrase, every construction, and also the order of the words employed by Caesar.*

In the winter of Brute's command, the Cymri attempted to dislodge, or at least to tame, the powerful race of Gogmagogi, a people who, dwelling near the point at which the river Plym enters the sea, made it a matter of national pride to create around them the widest desolation. Armed hordes annually went forth from among them, to harry the more flourishing, and—as Devonians go—more refined communities in the neighbourhood, who were unable to make head against their violence; while the rest who remained at home, to provide supplies for the raiders, took their turn in arms the following year. The proximity of this pugnacious people caused a complete stoppage of agriculture.

The Gogmagogi were a race of giants. Running wild from boyhood, following their own caprice, and knowing no obligation, only half-clad in their scanty garb of skins, their diet, composed mainly of animal food—for they were great in hunting—and their habit of daily exercise brought them to such a pitch of training that they were capable of the utmost exertions. Private property was unknown among them: so was trade, except with the purchasers of their spoils, and the providers of the costly French horses in which they delighted. There was no disgrace, to their minds, as bad as a poor-bred ill-made beast. They rode bare-back, quickly dismounting to fight on foot, while their horses stood stock-still, affording a ready refuge in case of need; and they would attack any number of saddle-using cavalry. Other imports they neither cared for nor allowed, implying that they weakened the power of endurance, and also because they feared ,to become Gallicised.

XLVIII.

*All the materials for this piece will be found in Caes.
Bell. Gall., Bk. IV., c. 17, which read carefully, noticing
every word and phrase, every construction, and also the order
of the words employed by Caesar.*

Hence he inferred that dignity and safety alike required
him to build a bridge, on such a plan that the greater the
strain it should be required to bear, the greater, owing to
excellence of materials and workmanship, should be its
cohesion. At reasonable distances in the river pairs of
vertical wooden piers, two feet square and four feet apart,
were dropped into their places by cranes and driven home
by pile-drivers, then coupled by cross-beams. Corresponding
pairs faced these, leaving an interspace of fifteen feet,
which was spanned by foot-and-a-half timbers : on them
rested girders, reaching from pier to pier, to the tops of
which they were also lashed on both sides by slanting
braces, thus distributing the pressure in opposite directions.
Joists of a length suitable to the interval between the
girders were then added, and floored with longitudinal
planking; while a rail of stakes and hurdles, on either
hand, ran the whole length of the bridge as a protection to
the crossing troops. The whole structure was buttressed by
tree-trunks, sharpened at the bottom, and fixed at a moderate inclination in the bed of the river, to prevent any
listing of the bridge in the direction of the set of the stream.
In this way, great as were the difficulties offered by the
breadth and rapidity of the river, he had resolved either to
cope with them, or else desist from any attempt to transport
his forces.

XLIX.

All the materials for this piece will be found in Caes. Bell. Gall., Bk. IV., cc. 20—26, which read carefully, noticing every word and phrase, every construction, and also the order of the words employed by Caesar.

The Admiral, not choosing that such trifling engagements should interfere with his design, moved on to the further haven, which offered the shortest sea-passage, and then waited a few days for the purpose of assembling his armament, as the fleet that had been ordered to be built in the previous summer had been wind-bound and prevented from coming into harbour. Meanwhile he mustered all his men-of-war from the neighbouring stations, and chartered transports sufficient, in his judgment, to carry a couple of regiments, together with a number of infantry mounted on well-trained chargers—an arm of the service which he generally employed with great effect. The more handy vessels he moored off the level and open shore; but the transports, owing to their burden, could only be stationed in deep water, where they rode at anchor. Then, a little before he intended to start, he gave the order to perform the evolution of embarkation and rapid disembarkation. Owing to the soldiers' ignorance of the locality and their hesitation when in the deeper water, it was performed in a rather slovenly manner. Observing this, he sent for his officers, partly to make them acquainted with his intentions, partly to give them a little salutary admonition.

L.

All the materials for this piece will be found in Caes. Bell. Gall., Bk. IV., cc. 20—26, which read carefully, noticing every word and phrase, every construction, and also the order of the words employed by Caesar.

[1] 'I observe,' said he, 'that your men have not shown their usual smartness and spirit, and consider it fortunate that this happened while we are still here, and before we have begun our enterprise. I recognise the magnitude of the difficulties : heavily accoutred soldiers, with their hands full, cannot be as steady in the water as if they were on dry land with their limbs free. Still you must understand that, more than other operations of war, naval evolutions, subject as they are to rapid and incalculable aberration, require to be executed upon the signal, punctually and simultaneously. Summer is nearly over and there is little chance of a campaign, as winters are early in these northern latitudes : yet even a simple visit in force to the island will I think be productive of good. It is an almost unknown region. An officer, on whose judgment I rely, commissioned to make as complete a survey as opportunities would allow him without leaving his ship, has inspected the coast, and reports the existence of harbours with accommodation for large sail. But, as even merchants are chary of risking their lives among these barbarians, he could bring back no information as to their numbers or military character. However, as I have now excellent sailing weather, with wind and tide in my favour, I am resolved to start Success ! Every man do his duty to his country !'

[1] Use *Oratio Obliqua* to the end of this piece.

LI.

All the materials for this piece will be found in Caes. Bell. Gall., Bk. IV., cc. 20—26, which read carefully, noticing every word and phrase, every construction, and also the order of the words employed by Caesar.

News of our plans must have been transmitted by the merchants; for when, about three o'clock in the afternoon, we made land, at a place not at all well fitted for disembarkation, we found the native forces displayed on a narrow line of cliffs, within spear's cast of the water; and the first few vessels were greeted as they approached with a bold flight of missiles. However the ships of war were rapidly brought up with the sweeps, and their unfamiliar appearance caused much alarm. When orders were given to dislodge the foe by a simultaneous discharge of weapons of every arm, unused to warfare of this description, they drew back in a body.

After some delay came a deputation, headed by a man who was evidently an influential personage. He offered an apology for their conduct: they were only savages, unacquainted with our manners; henceforth they would obey our sovereign dictation, and render hostages. The Admiral replied that they had acted disgracefully; yet, if they would undertake to send no more reinforcements to our enemies, he would accept their submission. He exhorted them, with liberal promises, to keep in the same mind, and bring over as many as they could of their neighbours; and then dismissed them.

LII.

All the materials for this piece will be found in Caes.
Bell. Gall., Bk. IV., cc. 26—31, *which read carefully, noticing*
every word and phrase, every construction, and also the order
of the words employed by Caesar.

Once only our old luck forsook us. We thought we were
armed against every contingency. The enemy had taken
their way back to their fields. Chieftains poured in every
day, without intermission, to sue for favour from the
Admiral, casting the blame for what had occurred upon the
multitude, begging pardon for their inadvertency, and offering abject submission; hostages were promised, and summoned even from far-off districts, and peace was thus an
accomplished fact. But, on the night of the full moon,
there occurred a very heavy spring tide, accompanied by a
sudden and violent storm. The ships, which had been
hauled over their anchors, were obliged, for fear of founder-
ing, to run before the wind, hoping to make some continental harbour; but, as they were undermanned, there was
little chance of managing them. Indeed they were unable
to keep a course, and drifted helplessly upon the shore,
rather more towards the west. Many of the vessels were
wrecked, as was inevitable; the crews of the others took to
the gigs and pinnaces, which in many cases were immediately swamped, or jumped overboard in a body.

LIII.

All the materials for this piece will be found in Caes. Bell. Gall., Bk. IV., cc. 26—31, which read carefully, noticing every word and phrase, every construction, and also the order of the words employed by Caesar.

The natives, who had secretly brought up their forces from the country, flocked to the beach. Familiar with every shoal, they rode down our men as, one by one, they got on dry land ; or in overpowering numbers surrounded small groups who were still hampered and unable to find a firm footing in the water, and discharged showers of missiles on all. The fighting on both sides was keen, as our men tried to prolong the engagement in order to give us a chance of coming to their relief.

The disaster to the fleet caused great consternation in the camp. The Admiral, at great personal risk, rushed to assist the distressed crews at the head of his troops, who, though unable to form companies or keep their ranks, charged the flank of the foe, and put them to rout.

Many ships had suffered severely—rigging and all ship furniture gone. As the hostile chiefs still hung about, talking together and calculating the smallness of the camp, the Admiral, though not quite sure of their plans, suspected conspiracy and rebellion, and an attempt to cut off his communications. Knowing that he must winter there, and had no winter supplies, he thought the best thing to be done was to use the timber and metal of the disabled vessels to repair some of the rest, and send these across for cargoes of provisions and ship-wright's materials. So smartly were his orders carried out, that very soon seven transports were made seaworthy.

LIV.

All the materials for this piece will be found in Caes. Bell. Gall., Bk. IV., cc. 32—38, which read carefully, noticing every word and phrase, every construction, and also the order of the words employed by Caesar.

To avoid the risk of a stormy passage during the equinox, the ships were despatched at once, and made their port safely; to return very soon and disembark the body of infantry referred to above, whose number had been doubled. These men were provided with chargers, and, by daily exercise, reached such a pitch of horsemanship, that they could pull up at full gallop, and wheel sharply round, even on a steep declivity. Slipping among the squadrons, or disordered lines, of an enemy, they could dismount and fight on foot : having a ready means of retreat to the main body, they escaped danger by their rapidity, and also by the novelty of their evolutions. In a word, they united the mobility of horse with the solidity of infantry.

A comparatively small number of these, on their way to relieve guard, observed an unusual cloud of dust, and saw a native driving a chariot in a most excited manner—even running along the pole and standing on the yoke. Fearing some revolutionary design or a repetition of the late accident, they strained every nerve in the direction lately taken by a foraging party. They arrived just in the nick of time, finding our men packed close together and under a heavy fire. The enemy fled to their old retreat in the dry parts of the marshes. Our men, after a brief breathing space, explained that, while engaged in reaping, they were set upon by marauders, who demanded their arms or their lives; they had formed square and defended themselves for more than five hours, though able only to keep their own ground.

LV.

All the materials for this piece will be found in Caes. Bell. Gall., Bk. V., cc. 1—11, which read carefully, noticing every word and phrase, every construction, and also the order of the words employed by Caesar.

After making the tour of the states and holding the customary annual courts, the spirited revolutionary found that public feeling ran high in his favour. His prestige, indeed, was overwhelming. Those who joined him from old association he put on their honour never to falter in their friendship. Leading citizens, who paid him the compliment of suing for personal favours, when required to pledge themselves by oath to remain firm in their allegiance, responded with enthusiasm. The throne was offered him, with absolute authority to shape his policy as time and circumstances should warrant. In a word the whole community seemed at his disposal, and there was nothing to deter him from his premeditated design.

Bidding his officers dock and repair the vessels previously provided in view of the civil war, he added some new ships after a model of his own. These were of broader beam than usual, and flatter-bottomed, for convenience of beaching, while a low free-board contributed to rapidity in loading. The task was painful and laborious; nevertheless the ship-wrights made such praiseworthy efforts, even working nightshifts, that in three months all were fully equipped and ready for sea, or so far advanced as to be fit for immediate launching. Complimenting the foremen, he ordered a further number of vessels of the class above described: while his fleet was swelled by transports and cargo-boats.

LVI.

All the materials for this piece will be found in Caes. Bell. Gall., Bk. V., cc. 1—11, which read carefully, noticing every word and phrase, every construction, and also the order of the words employed by Caesar.

Everything else postponed, that the summer might not be wasted, he resolved to raid upon the enemy's seaboard. Leaving a sufficient number of troops to protect the harbour, he proceeded in force to the point most convenient for crossing the strait—the passage being, indeed, not more than twenty-five miles. Here he gave orders to embark, hoping to take advantage both of the turn of the tide and of the south-westerly wind which generally blows, in these districts, during a large part of every season. The failure of the wind delayed their voyage, and it was not till noon that the island was reached, and an excellent landing-place found on a gently-shelving beach, free from rocks.

Large bands of natives had assembled, but, on his arrival, buried themselves in panic in the woods, the last stragglers only being in sight when the army was landed. Knowing he could not keep pace with the fugitives, he divided his forces into three parts, one of which he despatched on an excursion. After a considerable advance, they reached the woods, in front of which were a few skirmishers in loose order, with whom blows were interchanged; and a few prisoners were made, who were retained as hostages. From these he learned that the forest was of enormous size, reaching to the foot of the mountains; all avenues were choked by felled trees; while in the interior was an excellent natural fortification, improved by art, an earthwork being recently added. But, as he was unacquainted with the ground, and day was far spent, he called a halt and ordered a retreat.

LVII.

All the materials for this piece will be found in Caes. Bell. Gall., Bk. V., cc. 1—11, which read carefully, noticing every word and phrase, every construction, and also the order of the words employed by Caesar.

When he returned to the place where he had left his fleet at anchor, under the protection of his main force, he found a north-west gale blowing. Both cables and anchors threatened to give, and the pilots could not undertake to ride out the storm, but advised him to run for it. When he had put out to sea, a great many disasters occurred through collisions, especially among the vessels of this year's construction and the sloops, fitted out on private venture, which had attached themselves to the expedition. Many were lost; the greater number were carried out of their reckoning by the force of the tide, and, when day dawned, saw their own coasts far astern on the left quarter. Only by dint of incessant labour at the sweeps, the remnant managed to reach again the port of their departure.

Undeterred, the commander set about the repair of his fleet, which he saw was a possible though laborious task, as the fittings had to be brought from a long distance. But he found his popularity on the wane. The minds of all were occupied by their private disappointments; there was a general falling-off of the richer classes; and he saw his commands disregarded before his own eyes. This he took ill; but, the more easily to retain the allegiance of his followers and win them back individually, he gave out that he would use every means to make amends for all losses, and appointed a board of arbitration to assess the sums due for compensation.

LVIII.

All the materials for this piece will be found in Caes. Bell. Gall., Bk. V., cc. 1—11, *which read carefully, noticing every word and phrase, every construction, and also the order of the words employed by Caesar.*

Matters were aggravated by messages of excuse or remonstrance from men of position. They informed him that they were too aged for service, or bad sailors, or prevented by religious scruples. "He had himself to blame, if he was left in the lurch by the nobles : for none of his measures were national. Nor was it mere blindness made the populace slip away from him. The interruptions of incessant wars, the contentions of rival candidates for power, were not in the interests of the country, whose advantage they must consult. At any rate they could not confide the fortunes of the country to his honour merely.' When these discourses passed through his mind, he perceived their drift, and was grievously offended.

Still he attempted to solicit his supporters singly. He was met by flat refusals. All hope of successful entreaty lost, he blazed with increased resentment, and his passion rose to such a pitch that his actions became those of a madman. The matter called for public action : "he must be checked before he did the state a mischief.' He had started for the sea, when troops were sent to compel him to return. They found him in a state of absolute destitution. At first he protested that he was a free citizen, and appealed to their honour; but at length, refusing to obey and offering violence, he was surrounded and slain.

[1] Use *Oratio Obliqua.*

LIX.

All the materials for this piece will be found in Caes. Bell. Gall., Bk. V., cc. 12—23, *which read carefully, noticing every word and phrase, every construction, and also the order of the words employed by Caesar.*

As the result of our inquiries we found that the island is of a triangular shape, with a perimeter of seventeen hundred miles, the side which trends to the north being five hundred miles in length, and that which looks southwards, over an open sea, about seven hundred and fifty miles. Off the western coast lies another island, one half less, at much the same distance as the mainland. Half-way across are a number of islets, parted by extremely narrow strips of water. The climate on the seaboard is milder, with less severe frosts, than in the inland regions; which are densely wooded, with timber of every species familiar to us, especially beech and pine. The wilds, threaded only by narrow paths, shelter pretty considerable herds of cattle, of the continental type; but, according to the views of the natives, to taste flesh, or even milk, is irreligion, and the animals which they rear, such as hares or fowls, are kept as pets. The rivers are fordable, and that with difficulty, only in a few places, which are protected by lines of stakes; and even here no more than the head can be kept above water. It is reported that in mid-winter there is a month of unbroken night, when time can only be reckoned by water-clocks. The population is vast, the tribes naming themselves after the places from which they are traditionally said to have sprung. Clad in skins, stained blue, long-haired, unshorn except on the upper lip, they present in war a grisly appearance.

LX.

*All the materials for this piece will be found in Caes.
Bell. Gall., Bk. V., cc. 12—23, which read carefully, noticing
every word and phrase, every construction, and also the order
of the words employed by Caesar.*

Houses are not very frequent, as the people are free
rovers. Towns with them mean natural fortifications, in the
depths of intricate forests, strengthened, as a defence against
inroads, by mounds and moats. Most districts are shut out
from the use of the sea, and at the same time protected
from the violence of invaders. One corner, which pro-
duces tin and iron in small quantities—the only money
consists of iron nails—is visited by vessels, and possesses a
naval station.

A cloud of charioteers burst from the woods in which
they had been designedly hidden, and swooped upon the
troops landed by the first convoy. At such odds, retreat or
advance, in loose order, was equally fatal; so they remained
in solid formation round the standard, trusting to their supports, and the battle passed before their eyes. The ground
was unfavourable for cavalry evolutions; but relays constantly coming up from the videttes so thickly posted along
the route, and fresh men taking the place of those who were
fagged, they drove the enemy to headlong flight, without a
chance of recovery. After many disasters, the main forces
of the foe withdrew: the rest, angered at their desertion,
abandoned the river banks, and, while keeping clear of our
path, dogged our advance for a considerable time. It soon
became plain that the only damage to be done us was by

sudden sallies upon careless foragers; and they had to give up all hope of successful resistance. The only course left was to come to terms. Perceiving that what little summer remained would be wasted in procrastinations, we at once fixed a tribute, and, leaving a governor invested with absolute power, carried our forces back in two trips. Weighing anchor in perfectly smooth weather, all got across safely, not a ship missing or cast out of her course.

LXI.

*All the materials for this piece will be found in Caes.
Bell. Gall., Bk. VI., cc. 11—20, which read carefully, noticing
every word and phrase, every construction, and also the order
of the words employed by Caesar.*

While on this topic it seems not irrelevant to treat of the
few of most exalted rank, who possess supreme authority
over the others. They preside at religious functions, and
decide all questions of sacred ceremonial. To their absolute fiat ultimate reference is made in all measures or dis-
cussions of importance; they lay down for themselves the
laws of expediency, without sharing their confidence with
others, and pronounce their will only in congregation.
Sitting in consecrated places, they are completely irrespon-
sible, and are practically endowed with the powers and
privileges of the everlasting gods. Indeed it is alleged that
they do not really die, but are only subject to metempsycho-
sis. When a death occurs, a selection is made, by vote, out
of the most distinguished survivors, of a successor, who steps
into the vacant place, there to enjoy an enlarged prestige
and prerogative. In the ordinary concerns of life, they
entertain quite peculiar opinions : they deem it sacrilege for
the young to share their company in public—indeed they fly
their approach and conversation, as though they feared a mischief from their contagion. In this way they stimulate the
young to moral excellence.

LXII.

All the materials for this piece will be found in Caes. Bell. Gall., Bk. VI., cc. 11—20, which read carefully, noticing every word and phrase, every construction, and also the order of the words employed by Caesar.

Education is, by prescription, in the hands of these clergy. Large numbers of young men flock to one or two fixed localities, to pass through a course of higher instruction—some voluntarily, from a desire to learn, still more because they are sent by parents and guardians. The priests are handsomely endowed to make researches in cosmology, astronomy and the like, and lecture on the elements of the arts to the students ; who take copious notes, often in Greek characters, in order, no doubt, to prevent valuable information being disseminated among the vulgar. Reliance upon the safeguard of writing leads them to neglect the careful training of the memory: and persons have been known to spend twenty years in residence before completing their course—indeed, some retire unsuccessful. It is to be added that all who wish to study any branch of learning thoroughly, must go abroad to seek it on its native soil.

If it happen that some student or another shall have transgressed a judgment or decree of the authorities, or been remiss in his religious duties, although he may plead serious illness in excuse, or have fallen into some misdemeanour, or even if the matter have amounted to a suspicion, an inquisitorial examination takes place. In case of conviction, he is put in the category of abandoned criminals, outlawed, deprived of sustenance, and racked with agonies of suffering. In the absence of guilty persons, it is said that recourse has been had to the torture of the innocent.

LXIII.

All the materials for this piece will be found in Cacs. Bell. Gall., Bk. VI., cc. 11—20, which read carefully, noticing every word and phrase, every construction, and also the order of the words employed by Caesar.

Every knight, who wished to proclaim himself of noble lineage, surrounded himself, according to his rank and condition, with a multitude of vassals and retainers. In the event of war—an almost annual occurrence—these had to perform military functions, and passed their lives amid the dangers of the battle-field. Their will was never consulted; they were crushed by taxation; and indeed their seigneurs had over them the rights of masters over slaves, extending to the power of life and death. One sole privilege they enjoyed. On the birthdays of the illustrious, the commons, in sport, prepared funeral pageantries, on a scale—for their fashions—of sumptuous splendour, and burned in bonfires gigantic osier effigies, adding to the flames such articles as were supposed to be to the taste of the imaginary victim. This has been supposed to be a relic of the practice of human sacrifice.

Continual rivalries for supreme power arose among the highest nobility. From time to time some man, not content to play a secondary part in the state, would attempt to win over to himself the followings of his neighbours. Every city, every village, and even every family, was rent by faction; and the same condition applied to the whole community, which was split up into two hostile parties.

LXIV.

All the materials for this piece will be found in Cars. Bell. Gall., Bk. VI., cc. 11—20, which read carefully, noticing every word and phrase, every construction, and also the order of the words employed by Caesar.

Such was the state of affairs when the emperor landed. His arrival caused a revolution. Too weak in himself to contend against the powerful followings of the principal barons, he was led by necessity to appeal to the commons, whom he endeavoured to win over by promises of the most ruinous character.

[1] 'Why should the commons be kept in a state of bondage? Why swear homage to nobles, by whom they were cajoled and crushed and slain? Let them rally around him. All should hold the same honourable rank in his esteem, all should be men of worth and note; and he would enter upon no policy without inviting them to assist at his council. Stern justice could only be appeased by a life for a life: and all the nobility deserved immolation. But he would be satisfied with less. Let them secure by law that each noble should return an assessment of all property belonging to him, or accruing by way of dowry; let all properties be combined, a joint account kept, and the interest carefully collected, including arrears for past years. These sums should be devoted to public purposes, and would give a marked stimulus to profitable commercial activity. Let all therefore flock to his banner. He would provide them with means to repel all threatened wrongs. No commoner should ever lack help against the oppressor; and all the rights of the good old time should be restored, under happier conditions, fairer rule, and more faultless administration.'

[1] Use *Oratio Obliqua.*

LXV.

All the materials for this piece will be found in Caes. Bell. Gall., Bk. VI., cc. 21—28, which read carefully, noticing every word and phrase, every construction, and also the order of the words employed by Caesar.

From early boyhood they are inured to toil and hardship, it being thought that spare diet and habits of endurance tend to overcome sloth, to increase the stature, and to steel the sinews. Their only clothing consists of scanty leathern aprons, and they bathe freely in the coldest rivers. Safe as they are from any fear of sudden invasion, for they live in the midst of a desert of their own creation, they still pay attention to the exercises of war, in order to train the rising generation. There once was a time when they possessed the highest military repute, never knowing when they were beaten, and never rivalled, even in thought, by their neighbours. Larceny is no disgrace with them; yet the stranger is inviolate, and finds open house—if any man contravene this principle, he loses his character altogether. Flesh and cheese are the staple of their food; at their great feasts they drink milk, out of silver-capped horns, used in lieu of cups. Foreign luxuries, which might enlarge their comforts, are unknown; and their houses are built with little precaution against either heat or cold. In religion they are not very devout; yet they elect officers to sacrifice to the few gods they recognise, as well as to administer law in the cantons, and to settle disputes between the clans; and these men bear the highest name for integrity. Agriculture is neglected, owing to lack of soil. As landmarks and private estates are unknown, it is easy for the lower classes to match the noblest in wealth; and the commons are kept quiet by contentment.

LXVI.

All the materials for this piece will be found in Caes.
Bell. Gall., Bk. VI., cc. 21—28, which read carefully, noticing
every word and phrase, every construction, and also the order
of the words employed by Caesar.

Their main business is hunting, which has grown by use
into a passion. Every year they go to an immense forest,
which extends in breadth a ten days' journey—their only
mode of measuring distances—even for an active traveller
making straight for the river : thence it winds to the left, and
has never been explored to its remotest verge.

Most of the animals are little different from those found
elsewhere; but one species is noteworthy. The unicorn
is a creature somewhat larger than the ox, but of less bulk
than the elephant. From the middle of the forehead of the
male rises a single horn, particularly lofty and straight, the
female having rudimentary antlers. The general appearance
is that of a horse rearing on stiff and jointless legs : the skins
exhibit many shades of colour. The hunters carefully track
these beasts to their accustomed lairs—among clumps of
trees, against which they lean to sleep—and make burrows
beneath the roots; and when one of the creatures falls by
accident into the pit, it is unable to raise itself or get on
its feet again. To bring back home and make a public
display of great collections of these horns, in proof of prowess,
and to receive the plaudits of the multitude, is regarded as
the glory of manhood by the young bachelors of the tribe.

LXVII.

*All the materials for this piece will be found in Caes.
Bell. Gall., Bks. IV., c. 20—V., c. 23, VI., cc. 11—20, which
read carefully, noticing every word and phrase, every construction, and also the order of the words employed by Caesar.*

The captain states that about four months ago the ship
Nisero, after experiencing very severe weather, which made
it impossible for him to take observations, got out of its
course and was cast ashore on the coast of Acheen, in
the island of Sumatra. The captain and crew went on
land as soon as the state of the sea would permit, and were
at once confronted by a horde of natives, headed by the
Rajah of Tenom, who conducted them to a neighbouring
village of huts made of bamboo, with mat covering and open
sides. The whole of the crew, twenty-five in number, were
there put under guard, and allowed a meagre supply of raw
rice, night and morning, as their only food. From the sufferings imposed upon the captive sailors and the threatening
attitude of their captors, it appeared that the Rajah's people
sought to make this an opportunity of extorting some considerable ransom from the Dutch, with whom they have
long been on terms of resentment.

LXVIII.

All the materials for this piece will be found in Caes. Bell. Gall., Bks. IV., c. 20—V., c. 23, VI., cc. 11—20, which read carefully, noticing every word and phrase, every construction, and also the order of the words employed by Caesar.

After some delay the captain obtained permission to go on board the vessel, which at this time could perhaps with some management have been got off the rocks, but no sooner did he go on board than his guard and the other natives who accompanied him set about pillaging the ship. They took out everything movable, besides bringing all the clothing, stores, and a large portion of the cargo ashore in their boats. A distribution of this plunder was at once made among the Rajah's followers, and then, on account of the spreading of an alarm that the Dutch were attempting a rescue, the unfortunate captain and crew were marched into the interior of the island, single file, through jungle, often crossing rivers up to their necks in water. The procession was headed by the Rajah himself, and the vanguard was commanded by his chief fighting men. After marching about twenty miles, the party arrived at a place where rude huts were at once erected, consisting of the usual bamboo-stockade formation. Confined within a narrow space, the prisoners were closely watched, the Rajah himself taking a share in the patrol duty to guard them.

LXIX.

All the materials for this piece will be found in Caes. Bell. Gall., Bks. IV., c. 20—V., c. 23, VI., cc. 11—20, which read carefully, noticing every word and phrase, every construction, and also the order of the words employed by Caesar.

Through the effects of the abominable climate, anxiety of mind, and want of proper food, the sufferings of the crew now became aggravated, and several of them were seriously ill, including the mate, whose reason became affected by excessive hardship. As it appeared to the Dutch that pressure was necessary in order to bring the Rajah to his senses, an expedition was organised. Several Dutch war-vessels landed a body of troops on the coast, where a fight took place with the natives, who were armed with spears, and short native swords. After making a bold stand the natives retreated to the bush, pursued by the Dutch soldiers, who eventually came to the place where the prisoners had been confined, but the hut encampment was now vacated, the Rajah having gone off with his prisoners to the mountains. Finding further pursuit hopeless the Dutch returned to their vessels, and since then no forcible step has been taken to effect the rescue of the British captives. The captain contrived with difficulty to preserve his papers by binding them round his body underneath his clothing.

LXX.

Materials for this piece will be found in Caes. Bell. Gall., Bks. IV., c. 20—V., c. 23, VI., cc. 11—20, which read carefully, noticing every word and phrase, every construction, and also the order of the words employed by Caesar.

The Rajah is described as a man of imposing appearance, splendid physique, and muscular powers, but without much pretension to regal grandeur. He carries a magnificent scimitar with jewelled hilt, hanging from the sash tied round his waist. In his own hut was spread a carpet, and all who approached were compelled to take off their shoes in his presence. On his head the Rajah wears a turban entwined with silver ornaments, but his habitation is little better than that of his subjects, and he has none of the ordinary appliances of civilized life. In the march already described he was accompanied by five dusky wives. At Acheen the Dutch have a kind of garrison, but no strangers dare venture more than a mile or two beyond the fort. It is stated that on one occasion a friendly Rajah, professing to fear an attack from his neighbour, asked for the help of a small Dutch force. An officer and a guard of a few men were sent in compliance with this request, but no sooner did they go than they were at once massacred, and the body of the unfortunate officer was sent back frightfully mutilated. Extreme anxiety is felt as to the fate of the crew, who, according to the latest accounts, are all reported to be still alive.

LXXI.[1]

All the materials for this piece will be found in Caes. Bell. Gall., Bks. IV., c. 20—V., c. 23, VI., cc. 11—20, which read carefully, noticing every word and phrase, every construction, and also the order of the words employed by Caesar.

Nothing is known of the history of Britain till the invasion of the island by Julius Caesar in B.C. 55. The fabulous tale of the colonization of the island by Brute the Trojan, the great grandson of Æneas, and of his long list of descendants, does not require any serious refutation. The only certain means by which nations can indulge their curiosity in researches concerning their remote origin is to consider the language, manners, and customs of their ancestors, and to compare them with those of the neighbouring nations. There can be no doubt that the first inhabitants of Britain were a tribe of Celts, who peopled the island from the neighbouring continent. Their language was the same; their manners, their government, their superstition,—varied only by those small differences which time or a communication with the bordering nations must necessarily introduce. The inhabitants of the interior were said by tradition to have sprung from the soil; from which we can only infer that the earlier immigrations of the Celts took place long before the memory of man. Tacitus supposed that the red hair and large limbs of the Caledonians indicated a German origin; and that the dark com-

---

[1] Nos. LXXI. — LXXIX. are extracts, made by Mr Murray's kind permission, from the first chapter of 'The Student's Hume,' which gives an account of the Romans in Britain. I have found them to form a most useful group of recapitulatory exercises.

plexion of the Silures, their curly hair, and their position opposite to Spain, furnished grounds for believing that they descended from Iberian settlers from that country, but these were evidently mere conjectures, to which Tacitus himself seems not to have attached much importance, since he adds that upon a careful estimate of probabilities we must believe that the Gauls took possession of the neighbouring coast.

LXXII.

All the materials for this piece will be found in Caes. Bell. Gall., Bks. IV., c. 20—V., c. 23, VI., cc. 11—20, which read carefully, noticing every word and phrase, every construction, and also the order of the words employed by Caesar.

The connection of the Britons with the Celts of Gaul is shown by their common religion. Caesar, indeed, was of opinion that Druidism had its origin in Britain, and was transplanted thence into Gaul; and it is certain that in his time Britain was the chief seat of the religion and the principal school where it was taught. But this circumstance only shows that the common faith of the Celtic tribes had been preserved in its greatest purity by the remotest and most ancient of them, who had been driven by the tide of emigration to the western parts of the island. The religion of the Britons was one of the most considerable parts of their government, and the Druids, who were their priests, possessed great authority among them. Besides ministering at the altar and directing all religious duties, they presided over the education of youth; they enjoyed an immunity from war and taxes; they possessed both the civil and the criminal jurisdiction; they decided all controversies, among states as well as among private persons, and whoever refused to submit to their decrees was exposed to the most severe penalties. The sentence of excommunication was pronounced against him; he was forbidden access to the sacrifices or public worship; he was debarred all intercourse with his fellow citizens; he was refused the protection of the law; and death itself became an acceptable relief from the misery and infamy to which he was exposed. Thus the bands of government, which were naturally loose among that rude and turbulent people, were happily strengthened by the terrors of their superstition.

LXXIII.

All the materials for this piece will be found in Caes. Bell. Gall., Bks. IV., c. 20—V., c. 23, VI., 11—20, which read carefully, noticing every word and phrase, every construction, and also the order of the words employed by Caesar.

No species of superstition was ever more terrible than that of the Druids. Besides the severe penalties which it was in the power of the priests to inflict in this world, they inculcated the eternal transmigration of souls. They practised their rites in dark groves or other secret recesses; and in order to throw a greater mystery over their religion, they communicated their doctrines only to the initiated, and strictly forbade the committing of them to writing, lest they should at any time be exposed to the examination of the profane vulgar. In the ordinary concerns of life, however, they employed writing, their character being either Greek or a sort of hieroglyphics formed from the figures of plants. The Druids worshipped a plurality of gods, to which Caesar, after the Roman fashion, applies the names of the deities of his own country. The attributes of the god chiefly worshipped appear to have resembled those of Mercury. The principles which the Druids inculcated were piety towards the gods, charity towards man, and fortitude in suffering. They taught their disciples astronomy, or rather perhaps astrology, and magic, and trained them to acuteness in legal distinction; and a term of twenty years was commonly devoted to the acquisition of the knowledge which they imparted. They chose their own high-priest, but the election was frequently decided by arms.

LXXIV.

*All the materials for this piece will be found in Caes.
Bell. Gall., Bks. IV., c. 20—V., c. 23, VI., cc. 11—20, which
read carefully, noticing every word and phrase, every construction, and also the order of the words employed by Caesar.*

Human sacrifices formed one of the most terrible features
of the Druidical worship. The victims were generally criminals or prisoners of war, but, in default of these, innocent and
inoffending persons were sometimes immolated; and in the
larger sacrifices immense figures made of plaited osier were
filled with human beings and then set on fire. The spoils of
war were often devoted by the Druids to their divinities, and
they punished with the severest tortures whoever dared to
secrete any part of the consecrated offerings. These trea-
sures they kept in woods and forests, secured by no other
guard than the terrors of their religion; and this steady
conquest over human avidity may be regarded as more
signal than their prompting men to the most extraordinary
and most violent efforts. No idolatrous worship ever
attained such an ascendant over mankind as that of the
ancient Gauls and Britons; and the Romans, after their
conquest, finding it impossible to reconcile those nations to
the laws and institutions of their masters, while it maintained its authority, were at last obliged to abolish it by
penal statute; a violence which had never in any other
instance been practised by those tolerating conquerors.

After the Druids, the chief authority was possessed by
the equestrian order. The British bards were closely
connected with the Druids. They sung the genealogies of
their princes, and possessed lyric poetry as well as epic and
didactic, accompanying their songs with an instrument
called the *chrotta*.

LXXV.

*All the materials for this piece will be found in Caes.
Bell. Gall., Bks. IV., c. 20—V., c. 23, VI., cc. 11—20, which
read carefully, noticing every word and phrase, every construction, and also the order of the words employed by Caesar.*

The south-eastern parts of Britain had already before
the age of Caesar made the first and most requisite step
towards a civil settlement; and the Britons, by tillage and
agriculture, had there increased to a great multitude. The
other inhabitants of the island still maintained themselves
by pasture: they were clothed with skins of beasts: they
dwelt in round huts constructed of wood or reeds, which
they reared in the forests and marshes with which the
country was covered: they shifted easily their habitations
when actuated either by the hopes of plunder or the fear of
an enemy: the convenience of feeding their cattle was even a
sufficient motive for removing their seats; and as they were
ignorant of all the refinements of life their wants and their
possessions were equally scanty and limited.

The Britons tattooed their bodies and stained them blue
and green with woad; customs which were long retained
by the Picts. They wore checkered mantles like the Gauls
or Scottish highlanders; the waist was circled with a girdle,
and metal chains adorned the breast. The hair and mus-
tachio were suffered to grow, and a ring was worn on the
middle finger, after the fashion of the Gauls. Their arms
were a small shield, javelins, and a pointless sword.

LXXVI.

All the materials for this piece will be found in Caes. Bell. Gall., Bks. IV., c. 20—V., c. 23, VI., cc. 11—20, which read carefully, noticing every word and phrase, every construction, and also the order of the words employed by Caesar.

They fought from chariots having scythes affixed to the axles. The warrior drove the chariot, and was attended by a servant who carried his weapons. The dexterity of the charioteers excited the admiration of the Romans. They would urge their horses at full speed down the steepest hills or along the edge of the precipices, and check and turn them in full career. Sometimes they would run along the pole, or seat themselves on the yoke, and instantly, if necessary, regain the chariot. Frequently after breaking the enemy's ranks they would leap down and fight on foot; meanwhile the chariots were withdrawn from the fray, and posted in such a manner as to afford a secure retreat in case of need, thus enabling them to combine the rapid evolutions of cavalry with the steady firmness of infantry. The Britons had no fortresses, and their towns, if such a name can be applied to mere clusters of huts, were defended by their position in the centre of almost impenetrable forests, and by being surrounded with a deep ditch, and a fence or wall of felled trees. Each state was divided into factions within itself: it was agitated with jealousy or animosity against the neighbouring states: and while the arts of peace were yet unknown, wars were the chief occupation, and formed the chief object of ambition, among the people.

LXXVII.

All the materials for this piece will be found in Caes. Bell. Gall., Bks. IV., c. 20—V., c. 23, VI., cc. 11—20, which read carefully, noticing every word and phrase, every construction, and also the order of the words employed by Caesar.

Caesar, taking advantage of a short interval in his Gallic wars, invaded Britain with two legions in the year B.C. 55. The natives, informed of his intention, were sensible of the unequal contest, and endeavoured to appease him by submission, which, however, retarded not the execution of his design. After some resistance, he landed, as is supposed, at Deal; and having obtained several advantages over the Britons, and obliged them to promise hostages for their future obedience, he was constrained by the necessity of his affairs, and the approach of winter, to withdraw his forces into Gaul. The Britons relieved from the terror of his arms, neglected the performance of their stipulations; and that haughty conqueror resolved next summer (B.C. 54) to chastise them for this breach of treaty. He landed, apparently at the same spot, and unopposed, with above 20,000 men, and though he found a more regular resistance from the Britons, who had united under Caswallon, one of their petty princes, he discomfited them in every action. He advanced into the country and passed the Thames in the face of the enemy at a ford, in spite of the piles which Caswallon had caused to be driven into the bed of the river. The valiant defence of Caswallon was frustrated by the treacherous submission of the Trinobantes and other tribes.

LXXVIII.

All the materials for this piece will be found in Caes. Bell. Gall., Bks. IV., c. 20—V., c. 23, VI., cc. 11—20, which read carefully, noticing every word and phrase, every construction, and also the order of the words employed by Caesar.

After two years of peaceful administration, Suetonius Paulinus resolved on reducing the island of Mona, the chief seat of the Druids, which afforded a shelter to the disaffected Britons. The strait was crossed by the infantry in shallow vessels, whilst the cavalry either waded or swam. The Britons endeavoured to obstruct their landing on this sacred island, both by the force of their arms and the terror of their religion. The women and priests were intermingled with the soldiers upon the shore; and running about with flaming torches in their hands, and tossing their dishevelled hair, they struck greater terror into the astonished Romans by their howlings, cries, and execrations than the real danger from the armed forces was able to inspire. But Suetonius, exhorting his troops to disregard the menaces of a superstition which they despised, impelled them to the attack, drove the Britons off the field, burned the Druids in the same fires which those priests had prepared for their captive enemies, destroyed all the consecrated groves and altars; and having thus triumphed over the religion of the Britons, he thought his future progress would be easy in reducing the people to subjection. But he was disappointed in his expectations. The Britons taking advantage of his absence, were all in arms; and, headed by Boadicea, queen of the Iceni, whose daughter had been defiled and herself scourged with rods by the Roman tribunes, had already attacked with success several settlements of their insulting conquerors.

LXXIX.

*All the materials for this piece will be found in Caes.
Bell. Gall., Bks. IV., c. 20—V., c. 23, VI., cc. 11—20, which
read carefully, noticing every word and phrase, every construction, and also the order of the words employed by Caesar.*

This great commander, Julius Agricola, formed a regular
plan for subduing Britain and rendering the acquisition
useful to the conquerors. After subduing the Ordovices,
and again reducing Mona which had revolted, he carried
his victorious arms northwards. In the third year of his
government he marched as far as the Tay, where he
established garrisons; and in the following year he erected
a line of fortresses between the firths of Clyde and Forth.
He extended his conquests along the western shores of
Britain, and even meditated an expedition to Ireland. In
the sixth and seventh years of his administration he made
two incursions into Caledonia, in the latter of which he
gained a great and decisive victory over the inhabitants
under their leader Galgacus, at the foot of the Grampian
hills. One of the last acts of his government was to cause
his fleet to sail around Britain, starting from, and returning
to, the Portus Trutulensis. During these military enter-
prises he neglected not the arts of peace. He introduced
laws and civilization among the Britons, taught them to
desire and raise all the conveniences of life, reconciled them
to the Roman language and manners, instructed them in
letters and science, and employed every expedient to render
those chains which he had forged both easy and agreeable
to them. The inhabitants, having experienced how unequal
their own force was to resist that of the Romans, acquiesced
in the dominion of their masters, and were gradually incor-
porated as a part of that mighty empire.

APPENDIX.

The examples given below illustrate NOTE II. on Reported Speech, in conjunction with which they should be read, as they follow the same arrangement.   They are taken from The Gallic War itself, with the exception of three or four, which have been borrowed elsewhere, or specially constructed, in order to elucidate some quite classical usages that do not happen to occur in the Caesar.

A.

SUBORDINATE SENTENCES.

Instances of remarks of Caesar's own, interpolated in his report of a speech, and therefore presented in the Indicative form (v. p. xvii. ad init.), are

> Factum ejus hostis periculum patrum nostrorum memoria, cum... non minorem laudem exercitus quam ipse imperator meritus vide-*batur*.   B. G. I. 40.
> Germanos, qui cis Rhenum incol*unt*, sese cum his conjunxisse. B. G. II. 3.

A subordinate verb (ib.) is in the *first* person in

> Nos esse iniquos, quod in suo jure se interpellaremus.   B. G. I. 44.

SCHEMA I.

SUBORDINATE SENTENCES.

Oratio Recta.	*Oratio Obliqua.*

PRES. INDIC.

Quod vestra victoria tam inso-lenter gloria*mini*...eodem pertinet.

Quod sua victoria tam insolenter gloria*rentur*...eodem pertinere. B. G. I. 14.

Hoc mihi minus dubitationis datur quod has res...memoria ten*eo*.

Eo sibi minus dubitationis dari quod eas res...memoria ten*eret*. B. G. I. 14.

Propterea quod ipse meae civi-tatis imperium obtenturus *sum*.

Propterea quod ipse suae civi-tatis imperium obtenturus *esset*. B. G. I. 3.

PRES. SUBJ.

Mihi autem mirum videtur quid in mea Gallia...populo Romano negotii *sit*.

Sibi autem mirum videri quid in sua Gallia...populo Romano negotii *esset*. B. G. I. 34.

FUT. INDIC.

Cum voles, congredere.

Cum vellet congrederetur. B. G. I. 36.

PRES. INDIC.

De hac, quam hab*eo*, gratia despero.

De ea, quam hab*eat*†, gratia desperare. B. G. I. 18.

PRES. SUBJ.

Cum haec ita *sint*, tamen si obsides a vobis *dentur*, uti haec, quae pollic*emini*, vos facturos in-telliga*m*...ego vobiscum pacem faciam.

Cum ea ita *sint*†, tamen si ob-sides ab iis *dentur*, uti ea, quae pollice*antur*, facturos intellega*t*... sese cum iis pacem esse facturum. B. G. I. 14.

S.   8

FUT. INDIC.

Nisi subsidium mihi submitt*etur*, ego diutius sustinere non possum.

Nisi subsidium sibi submitta-tur†, sese diutius sustinere non posse. B. G. II. 6.

PERF. INDIC.

Hoc gravius fero, quo minus merito populi Romani accid*erunt*.

Eo gravius ferre, quo minus merito populi Romani accid*issent*. B. G. I. 14.

PERF. SUBJ.

Ut omni tempore totius Galliae principatum Aedui tenu*erint* prius etiam quam nostram amicitiam appetierunt.

Ut omni tempore totius Galliae principatum Aedui tenu*issent* prius etiam quam nostram amicitiam appetiissent. B. G. I. 43.

COMPL. FUT.

Non est fas vos superare si ante novam lunam praelio contend-*eritis*.

Non esse fas Germanos superare si ante novam lunam praelio contend*issent*. B. G. I. 50.

Laboramus ne haec, quae dixe-*rimus*, enuntientur.

Laborare ne ea, quae dix*issent*, enuntiarentur. B. G. I. 31.

PERF. INDIC.

Ob hanc rem, quam diu pot*ui*, tacui.

Ob eam rem, quam diu potu-*erit*†, tacuisse. B. G. I. 17.

PERF. SUBJ.

Ita nos meriti sumus ut...oppida expugnari non debu*erint*.

Ita se...meritos esse ut...oppida expugnari non debu*erint*†. B. G. I. 11.

Intellego quanto hoc cum periculo fec*erim*.

Intellegere sese quanto id cum periculo fec*erit*†. B. G. I. 17.

COMPL. FUT.

In eos omnia exempla cruciatusque edit, si qua res non ad nutum...facta *erit*.

In eos omnia exempla cruciatusque edere, si qua res non ad nutum...facta *sit*†. B. G. I. 31.

IMPERF. INDIC. AND SUBJ.

Sed hoc deceptus est populus Romanus quod neque commissum a se intelle*gebat* quare tim*eret*, neque sine causa timendum puta*bat*.

Sed eo deceptum quod neque commissum a se intelleg*eret* quare tim*eret*, neque sine causa timendum put*aret*. B. G. I. 14.

PLUPERF. INDIC.

Cum ii, qui flumen transi*erant*, suis auxilium ferre non poterant.

Cum ii, qui flumen trans*issent*, suis auxilium ferre non possent. B. G. I. 13.

Qui...plurimum ante in Gallia potuerant, coacti sunt...obsides dare.

Qui...plurimum ante in Gallia potuissent, coactos esse...obsides dare. B. G. I. 31.

PLUPERF. SUBJ.

Qui si alicujus injuriae sibi conscius *fuisset*, non fuit difficile cavere.

Qui si alicujus injuriae sibi conscius *fuisset*, non fuisse difficile cavere. B. G. I. 14.

PLUPERF. SUBJ. IN DEPENDENT HYPOTHESIS.

Subibat cogitatio animum, *quonam modo* tolerabilis *futura* Etruria *fuisset*, si quid in Samnio adversi evenisset. LIVY, X. 45.

Subiisse cogitationem animum, *quonam modo* tolerabilis *futura* Etruria *fuisset*, si quid in Samnio adversi evenisset.

Virgines eo cursu...se proripuerunt, *ut*, si effugium patuisset in publicum, imple*turae* urbem tumultu *fuerint*. LIVY, XXIV. 26.

Virgines eo cursu...se proripuisse, *ut*, si effugium patuisset in publicum, imple*turae* urbem tumultu *fuerint*.

APPENDIX.

B.

PRINCIPAL SENTENCES.

SCHEMA II.

PRINCIPAL STATEMENTS.

Oratio Recta.   *Oratio Obliqua.*

PRES. INDIC.
Perfacile factu *est* conata per-
ficere.

Perfacile factu *esse* conata per-
ficere. B. G. I. 3.

FUT. INDIC.
Ego vobiscum pacem fac*iam.*

Sese cum iis pacem *esse facturum.*
B. G. I. 14.

Tibi nihil noc*ebitur.*

Ipsi nihil noc*itum iri.* B. G. V.
36.

COMPL. FUT.
Cum tu haec leges, ego illum
fortasse conven*ero.* CICERO, *ad
Att.* IX. 15.

Cum is ea legeret, se illum fortasse conven*turum fuisse.*

PERF. INDIC.
His rebus et suam rem famili-
arem au*xit.*

His rebus et suam rem famili-
arem au*xisse.* B. G. I. 18.

Nos ne obsidibus quidem datis
pacem Ariovisti redimere pot*ui-
mus.*

Sese ne obsidibus quidem datis
pacem Ariovisti redimere pot*uisse.*
B. G. I. 37.

IMPERF. INDIC.
Ariovistus, me consule, cupidis-
sime populi Romani amicitiam
appet*ebat.*

Ariovistum, se consule, cupidis-
sime populi Romani amicitiam
appet*iisse.* B. G. I. 40.

PLUPERF. INDIC.
Nos cum...multos annos conten-
debamus, factum *erat* ut...Germani
arcesserentur.

Hi cum...multos annos conten-
derent, factum *esse* ut...Germani
arcesserentur. B. G. I. 31.

Inceptives, having no future participle, require a periphrasis :—

Oratio Recta: "Frigus," inquit, "mitescet." *Oratio Obliqua*: Fore ut frigus mitesceret.

This is also frequent with *passive* verbs.

Futurum esse paucis annis uti omnes ex Galliae finibus pellerentur. B. G. I. 31.

Qua ex re futurum uti totius Galliae animi a se averterentur. B. G. I. 20.

β.

(i)

DIRECT QUESTIONS IN THE FIRST OR THIRD PERSON.

Oratio Recta.

INDICATIVE.

Num etiam recentium injuriarum...memoriam deponere possum?

Quid *est* levius aut turpius quam auctore hoste de summis rebus capere consilium?

SUBJUNCTIVE.

Quod vero ad amicitiam populi Romani attulerant, id iis eripi quis pati *possit?*

Cur hunc tam temere quisquam ab officio discessurum judic*et?*

Quis hoc sibi persuad*eat?*...Consilium quem hab*eat* exitum?

Oratio Obliqua.

Num etiam recentium injuriarum...memoriam deponere *posse?* B. G. I. 14.

Quid *esse* levius aut turpius quam auctore hoste de summis rebus capere consilium? B. G. V. 28.

Quod vero ad amicitiam populi Romani attulissent, id iis eripi quis pati *posset?* B. G. I. 43.

Cur hunc tam temere quisquam ab officio discessurum judic*aret?* B. G. I. 40.

Quis hoc sibi persuad*eret?*...Consilium quem hab*eret* exitum? B. G. V. 29.

(ii)

SCHEMA III.

Direct Questions in the Second Person.

Oratio Recta.	*Oratio Obliqua.*
Pres. Indic.	
Cur de vestra virtute aut de mea diligentia desper*atis*? or,	Cur de sua virtute aut de ipsius diligentia desper*arent*? B. G. I. 40.
Pres. Subj.	
...desper*etis*?	(*Here we might also have had* †desper*ent*.)
Perf. Indic.	
Cur desper*avistis*?	Cur desperassent? (†desper*arint*).
Fut. Indic.	
Cur desper*abitis*?	Cur desper*aturi essent*? (or †*sint*).
Compl. Fut.	
Cur despera*veritis*?	Cur despera*turi fuissent*? (or †*fuerint*)
Imperf.	
Cur {desper*abant*? / desper*arent*?}	Cur desper*arent*?
Pluperf.	
Cur {desper*averant*? / desper*assent*?}	Cur desper*assent*?

γ.

Oratio Recta.	*Oratio Obliqua.*
Si quid vultis, ad Idus Apriles revert*imini*.	Si quid vellent, ad Idus Apriles revert*erentur*. B. G. I. 7.
Reminis*cere* veteris incommodi.	Reminis*ceretur* veteris incommodi. B. G. I. 13.
Ne nos despe*xeris*.	Ne ipsos desp*iceret*. B. G. I. 13.

Si velis tuos recipere, obsides nobis remitt*e*.

Si velit suos recipere, obsides sibi remitt*at*†. B.G. III. 8.

In consilio capiendo omnem Galliam respicia*mus*. B.G. VII. 77.

In consilio capiendo omnem Galliam sibi respiciendam esse (*or* respiciendum).

ϵ.

SCHEMA IV.

HYPOTHESES.

Oratio Recta.	*Oratio Obliqua.*

PRES. ACTIVE.

Si possim, pugn*em*.

Quod si te interfecerim, multis ego gratum fac*iam*.

Si posset, pugn*aturum fuisse.*

Quod si eum interfecerit, multis sese...gratum *esse*† *facturum.* B.G. I. 44.

Si vim facere conemini, prohib*ebo*.

Si vim facere conentur† prohib*iturum.* B.G. I. 8.

PRES. PASSIVE.

Si adsis, Ilium non oppugn*etur*.

Si is adesset, *futurum fuisse ut* Ilium non oppugn*aretur.* Or,

Si is adsit†, *fore ut* Ilium non oppugn*etur.*

But we find the Future Passive also, as

Si suae saluti consulant...dignitate spoli*entur*.

Si suae saluti consulant†...dignitate spoli*atum iri.* B.G. VII. 66.

IMPERF. ACT.

Si quid mihi a te opus esset, ego ad te venirem.

Si quid ipsi a Caesare opus esset, sese ad eum ven*turum fuisse.* B. G. I. 34.

Neque Eburones, si ille adesset, tanta cum contemptione nostri ad castra ven*irent*.

Neque Eburones, si ille adesset, tanta cum contemptione nostri ad castra ven*turos esse.* B. G. V. 29.

IMPERF. ACT.

Tum si dicerem, non audi*rer*. Cic. *pro Cl.* XXIX.

Tum si diceret, *futurum fuisse ut* non audi*retur*.

PLUPERF. ACT.

Neque aliter Carnutes interfici-endi Tasgetii consilium *cepissent*.

Neque aliter Carnutes inter-ficiendi Tasgetii consilium *fuisse capturos*. B. G. V. 29.

Qui si alicujus injuriae sibi con-scius fuisset, non *fuisset* (*where* fuit *could stand*) difficile cavere.

Qui si alicujus injuriae sibi con-scius fuisset, non *fuisse* difficile cavere. B. G. I. 14.

PLUPERF. PASS.

Quorum si aetas potuisset esse longinquior...omni doctrina homi-num vita erudi*ta esset*.

Quorum si aetas potuisset esse longinquior *futurum fuisse ut*... omni doctrina hominum vita eru-di*retur*. Cic. *Tusc.* XXVIII. 69.[1]

[1] Quoted from Roby, L. G. 1790.

CAMBRIDGE: PRINTED BY C. J. CLAY, M.A. & SON, AT THE UNIVERSITY PRESS.

A CATALOGUE

OF

CLASSICAL WORKS

PUBLISHED BY

MACMILLAN AND CO., LONDON,

COMPRISING

1. ELEMENTARY CLASSICS, for Beginners.
2. THE CLASSICAL SERIES, for Schools and Colleges.
3. THE CLASSICAL LIBRARY, for Higher Students
   (*a*) TEXTS ; (*b*) TRANSLATIONS.
4. WORKS ON GRAMMAR, COMPOSITION, & PHILOLOGY.
5. WORKS ON ANTIQUITIES, ANCIENT HISTORY, & ANCIENT PHILOSOPHY.
6. GREEK TESTAMENT.

CONTENTS.

29 AND 30, BEDFORD STREET, COVENT GARDEN, LONDON, W.C., *October*, 1886.

CLASSICS.

ELEMENTARY CLASSICS.

18mo, Eighteenpence each.

THIS SERIES FALLS INTO TWO CLASSES—

(1) First Reading Books for Beginners, provided not only with **Introductions and Notes**, but with **Vocabularies**, and in some cases with **Exercises** based upon the Text.

(2) Stepping-stones to the study of particular authors, intended for more advanced students who are beginning to read such authors as Terence, Plato, the Attic Dramatists, and the harder parts of Cicero, Horace, Virgil, and Thucydides.

These are provided with Introductions and Notes, **but no Vocabulary.** The Publishers have been led to provide the more strictly Elementary Books with Vocabularies by the representations of many teachers, who hold that beginners do not understand the use of a Dictionary, and of others who, in the case of middle-class schools where the cost of books is a serious consideration, advocate the Vocabulary system on grounds of economy. It is hoped that the two parts of the Series, fitting into one another, may together fulfil all the requirements of Elementary and Preparatory Schools, and the Lower Forms of Public Schools.

b 2

The following Elementary Books, with Introductions, Notes, **and Vocabularies**, and in some cases with **Exercises**, are either ready or in preparation:—

Aeschylus.—PROMETHEUS VINCTUS. Edited by Rev. H. M. STEPHENSON, M.A. [Ready.

Cæsar.—THE GALLIC WAR. BOOK I. Edited by A. S. WALPOLE, M.A. [Ready.

THE INVASION OF BRITAIN. Being Selections from Books IV. and V. of the "De Bello Gallico." Adapted for the use of Beginners. With Notes, Vocabulary, and Exercises, by W. WELCH, M.A., and C. G. DUFFIELD, M.A. [Ready.

THE GALLIC WAR. BOOKS II. AND III. Edited by the Rev. W. G. RUTHERFORD, M.A., LL.D., Head-Master of Westminster School. [Ready.

THE GALLIC WAR. BOOK IV. Edited by C. BRYANS, M.A., Assistant-Master at Dulwich College. Immediately.

THE GALLIC WAR. SCENES FROM BOOKS V. AND VI. Edited by C. COLBECK, M.A., Assistant-Master at Harrow; formerly Fellow of Trinity College, Cambridge. [Ready.

THE GALLIC WAR. BOOKS V. AND VI. (separately). By the same Editor. [In preparation.

Cicero.—DE SENECTUTE. Edited by E. S. SHUCKBURGH, M.A., late Fellow of Emmanuel College, Cambridge. [Ready.

DE AMICITIA. By the same Editor. [Ready.

STORIES OF ROMAN HISTORY. Adapted for the Use of Beginners. With Notes, Vocabulary, and Exercises, by the Rev. G. E. JEANS, M.A., Fellow of Hertford College, Oxford, and A. V. JONES, M.A., Assistant-Masters at Haileybury College. [Ready.

Eutropius.—Adapted for the Use of Beginners. With Notes, Vocabulary, and Exercises, by WILLIAM WELCH, M.A., and C. G. DUFFIELD, M.A., Assistant-Masters at Surrey County School, Cranleigh. [Ready.

Homer.—ILIAD. BOOK I. Edited by Rev. JOHN BOND, M.A., and A. S. WALPOLE, M.A. [Ready.

ILIAD. BOOK XVIII. THE ARMS OF ACHILLES. Edited by S. R. JAMES, M.A., Assistant-Master at Eton College. [Ready.

ODYSSEY. BOOK I. Edited by Rev. JOHN BOND, M.A. and A. S. WALPOLE, M.A. [Ready.

Horace.—ODES. BOOKS I.—IV. Edited by T. E. PAGE, M.A., late Fellow of St. John's College, Cambridge; Assistant-Master at the Charterhouse. Each 1s. 6d. [Ready.

Livy.—BOOK I. Edited by H. M. STEPHENSON, M.A., Head Master of St. Peter's School, York. [Ready.

Livy.—THE HANNIBALIAN WAR. Being part of the XXI. AND XXII. BOOKS OF LIVY, adapted for the use of beginners, by G. C. MACAULAY, M.A., Assistant-Master at Rugby ; formerly Fellow of Trinity College, Cambridge. [*Ready.*

THE SIEGE OF SYRACUSE. Being part of the XXIV. AND XXV. BOOKS OF LIVY, adapted for the use of beginners. With Notes, Vocabulary, and Exercises, by GEORGE RICHARDS, M.A., and A. S. WALPOLE, M.A. [*Ready.*

Lucian.—EXTRACTS FROM LUCIAN. Edited, with Notes, Exercises, and Vocabulary, by Rev. JOHN BOND, M.A., and A. S. WALPOLE, M.A. [*Ready.*

Nepos.—SELECT LIVES OF CORNELIUS NEPOS. Edited for the use of beginners with Notes, Vocabulary and Exercises, by G. S. FARNELL, M.A. [*Nearly ready.*

Ovid.—SELECTIONS. Edited by E. S. SHUCKBURGH, M.A. late Fellow and Assistant-Tutor of Emmanuel College, Cambridge. [*Ready.*

ELEGIAC SELECTIONS. Arranged for the use of Beginners with Notes, Vocabulary, and Exercises, by H. WILKINSON, M.A. [*In preparation.*

Phædrus.—SELECT FABLES. Adapted for the Use of Beginners. With Notes, Exercises, and Vocabularies, by A. S. WALPOLE, M.A. [*Ready.*

Thucydides.—THE RISE OF THE ATHENIAN EMPIRE. BOOK I. CC. LXXXIX. — CXVII. AND CXXVIII. — CXXXVIII. Edited with Notes, Vocabulary and Exercises, by F. H. COLSON, M.A., Senior Classical Master at Bradford Grammar School ; Fellow of St. John's College, Cambridge. [*Ready.*

Virgil.—ÆNEID. BOOK I. Edited by A. S. WALPOLE, M.A. [*Ready.*

ÆNEID. BOOK V. Edited by Rev. A. CALVERT, M.A., late Fellow of St. John's College, Cambridge. [*Ready.*

SELECTIONS. Edited by E. S. SHUCKBURGH, M.A. [*Ready.*

Xenophon.—ANABASIS. BOOK I. Edited by A. S. WALPOLE, M.A. [*Ready.*

SELECTIONS FROM THE CYROPÆDIA. Edited, with Notes, Vocabulary, and Exercises, by A. H. COOKE, M.A., Fellow and Lecturer of King's College, Cambridge. [*Ready.*

The following more advanced Books, with Introductions and Notes, **but no Vocabulary,** are either ready, or in preparation :—

Cicero.—SELECT LETTERS. Edited by Rev. G. E. JEANS, M.A., Fellow of Hertford College, Oxford, and Assistant-Master at Haileybury College. [*Ready.*

Euripides.—HECUBA. Edited by Rev. JOHN BOND, M A. and A. S. WALPOLE, M.A.   [*Ready*.

Herodotus.—SELECTIONS FROM BOOKS VI. AND VII., THE EXPEDITION OF XERXES. Edited by A. H. COOKE, M.A., Fellow and Lecturer of King's College, Cambridge. [*Ready*.

Horace. — SELECTIONS FROM THE SATIRES AND EPISTLES. Edited by Rev. W. J. V. BAKER, M.A., Fellow of St. John's College, Cambridge ; Assistant-Master in Marlborough College.   [*Ready*.
SELECT EPODES AND ARS POETICA. Edited by H. A. DALTON, M.A., formerly Senior Student of Christchurch ; Assistant-Master in Winchester College.   [*Ready*.

Plato.—EUTHYPHRO AND MENEXENUS. Edited by C. E. GRAVES, M.A., Classical Lecturer and late Fellow of St. John's College, Cambridge.   [*Ready*.

Terence.—SCENES FROM THE ANDRIA. Edited by F. W. CORNISH, M.A., Assistant-Master at Eton College.   [*Ready*.

The Greek Elegiac Poets.— FROM CALLINUS TO CALLIMACHUS. Selected and Edited by Rev. HERBERT KYNASTON, D.D., Principal of Cheltenham College, and formerly Fellow of St. John's College, Cambridge.   [*Ready*.

Thucydides.—BOOK IV. CHS. I.—XLI. THE CAPTURE OF SPHACTERIA. Edited by C. E. GRAVES, M.A. [*Ready*.

Virgil.—GEORGICS. BOOK II. Edited by Rev. J. H. SKRINE, M.A., late Fellow of Merton College, Oxford ; Assistant-Master at Uppingham.   [*Ready*.
*** *Other Volumes to follow.*

CLASSICAL SERIES
FOR COLLEGES AND SCHOOLS.

Fcap. 8vo.

Being select portions of Greek and Latin authors, edited with Introductions and Notes, for the use of Middle and Upper forms of Schools, or of candidates for Public Examinations at the Universities and elsewhere.

Æschines.— IN CTESIPHONTEM. Edited by Rev. T. GWATKIN, M.A., late Fellow of St. John's College, Cambridge.
[*In the press.*

Æschylus. — PERSÆ. Edited by A. O. PRICKARD, M.A. Fellow and Tutor of New College, Oxford. With Map. 3s. 6d.

Andocides.—DE MYSTERIIS. Edited by W. J. HICKIE, M.A., formerly Assistant Master in Denstone College. 2s. 6d.

Cæsar.—THE GALLIC WAR. Edited, after Kraner, by Rev. JOHN BOND, M.A., and A. S. WALPOLE, M.A. [In the press.

Catullus.—SELECT POEMS. Edited by F. P. SIMPSON, B.A., late Scholar of Balliol College, Oxford. New and Revised Edition. 5s. The Text of this Edition is carefully adapted to School use.

Cicero.—THE CATILINE ORATIONS. From the German of KARL HALM. Edited, with Additions, by A. S. WILKINS, M.A., LL.D., Professor of Latin at the Owens College, Manchester, Examiner of Classics to the University of London. New Edition. 3s. 6d.

PRO LEGE MANILIA. Edited, after HALM, by Professor A. S. WILKINS, M.A., LL.D. 2s. 6d.

THE SECOND PHILIPPIC ORATION. From the German of KARL HALM. Edited, with Corrections and Additions, by JOHN E. B. MAYOR, Professor of Latin in the University of Cambridge, and Fellow of St. John's College. New Edition, revised. 5s.

PRO ROSCIO AMERINO. Edited, after HALM, by E. H. DONKIN, M.A., late Scholar of Lincoln College, Oxford; Assistant-Master at Sherborne School. 4s. 6d.

PRO P. SESTIO. Edited by Rev. H. A. HOLDEN, M.A., LL.D., late Fellow of Trinity College, Cambridge; and late Classical Examiner to the University of London. 5s.

Demosthenes.—DE CORONA. Edited by B. DRAKE, M.A., late Fellow of King's College, Cambridge. New and revised Edition. 4s. 6d.

ADVERSUS LEPTINEM. Edited by Rev. J. R. KING, M.A., Fellow and Tutor of Oriel College, Oxford. 4s. 6d.

THE FIRST PHILIPPIC. Edited, after C. REHDANTZ, by Rev. T. GWATKIN, M.A., late Fellow of St. John's College, Cambridge. 2s. 6d.

IN MIDIAM. Edited by Prof. A. S. WILKINS, LL.D., and HERMAN HAGER, Ph.D., of the Owens College, Manchester. [In preparation.

Euripides.—HIPPOLYTUS. Edited by J. P. MAHAFFY, M.A., Fellow and Professor of Ancient History in Trinity College, Dublin, and J. B. BURY, Fellow of Trinity College, Dublin. 3s. 6d.

Euripides.—MEDEA. Edited by A. W. VERRALL, M.A., Fellow and Lecturer of Trinity College, Cambridge. 3s. 6d.

IPHIGENIA IN TAURIS. Edited by E. B. ENGLAND, M.A., Lecturer at the Owens College, Manchester. 4s. 6d.

Herodotus.—BOOKS VII. AND VIII. Edited by Rev. A. II. COOKE, M.A., Fellow of King's College, Cambridge. [*In prep.*

Homer.—ILIAD. BOOKS I., IX., XI., XVI.—XXIV. THE STORY OF ACHILLES. Edited by the late J. H. PRATT, M.A., and WALTER LEAF, M.A., Fellows of Trinity College, Cambridge. 6s.

ODYSSEY. BOOK IX. Edited by Prof. JOHN E. B. MAYOR. 2s. 6d.

ODYSSEY. BOOKS XXI.—XXIV. THE TRIUMPH OF ODYSSEUS. Edited by S. G. HAMILTON, B.A., Fellow of Hertford College, Oxford. 3s. 6d.

Horace.—THE ODES. Edited by T. E. PAGE, M.A., formerly Fellow of St. John's College, Cambridge; Assistant-Master at Charterhouse. 6s. (BOOKS I., II., III., and IV. separately, 2s. each.)

THE SATIRES. Edited by ARTHUR PALMER, M.A., Fellow of Trinity College, Dublin; Professor of Latin in the University of Dublin. 6s.

THE EPISTLES AND ARS POETICA. Edited by A S. WILKINS, M.A., LL.D., Professor of Latin in Owens College, Manchester; Examiner in Classics to the University of London. 6s.

Isaeos.—THE ORATIONS. Edited by WILLIAM RIDGEWAY, M.A., Fellow of Caius College, Cambridge; and Professor of Greek in the University of Cork. [*In preparation.*

Juvenal. THIRTEEN SATIRES. Edited, for the Use of Schools, by E. G. HARDY, M.A., Head Master of Grantham Grammar School; late Fellow of Jesus College, Oxford. 5s.
The Text of this Edition is carefully adapted to School use.

SELECT SATIRES. Edited by Professor JOHN E. B. MAYOR. X. AND XI. 3s. 6d. XII.—XVI. 4s. 6d.

Livy.—BOOKS II. AND III. Edited by Rev. H. M. STEPHENSON, M.A., Head-Master of St. Peter's School, York. 5s.

BOOKS XXI. AND XXII. Edited by the Rev. W. W. CAPES, M.A., Reader in Ancient History at Oxford. Maps. 5s.

Livy.—BOOKS XXIII AND XXIV. Edited by G. C. MACAULAY, M.A., Assistant-Master at Rugby. With Maps. 5*r*.

THE LAST TWO KINGS OF MACEDON. SCENES FROM THE LAST DECADE OF LIVY. Selected and Edited, with Introduction and Notes, by F. H .RAWLINS, M.A., Fellow of King's College, Cambridge; and Assistant-Master at Eton. With Maps. [*Nearly ready.*

Lucretius. BOOKS I.—III. Edited by J. H. WARBURTON LEE, M.A., late Scholar of Corpus Christi College, Oxford, and Assistant-Master at Rossall. 4*s*. 6*d*.

Lysias.—SELECT ORATIONS. Edited by E. S. SHUCKBURGH, M.A., late Assistant-Master at Eton College, formerly Fellow and Assistant-Tutor of Emmanuel College, Cambridge. New Edition, revised. 6*s*.

Martial. — SELECT EPIGRAMS. Edited by Rev. H. M. STEPHENSON, M.A. 6*s*.

Ovid.—FASTI. Edited by G. H. HALLAM, M.A., Fellow of St. John's College, Cambridge, and Assistant-Master at Harrow. With Maps. 5*s*.

HEROIDUM EPISTULÆ XIII. Edited by E. S. SHUCKBURGH, M.A. 4*s*. 6*d*.

METAMORPHOSES. BOOKS XIII. AND XIV. Edited by C. SIMMONS, M.A. [*Nearly ready.*

Plato.—MENO. Edited by E. S. THOMPSON, M.A., Fellow of Christ's College, Cambridge. [*In preparation.*

APOLOGY AND CRITO. Edited by F. J. H. JENKINSON, M.A., Fellow of Trinity College, Cambridge. [*In preparation.*

THE REPUBLIC. BOOKS I.—V. Edited by T. H. WARREN, M.A., President of Magdalen College, Oxford. [*In the press.*

Plautus.—MILES GLORIOSUS. Edited by R. Y. TYRRELL. M.A., Fellow of Trinity College, and Regius Professor of Greek in the University of Dublin. Second Edition Revised. 5*s*.

AMPHITRUO. Edited by ARTHUR PALMER, M.A., Fellow of Trinity College and Regius Professor of Latin in the University of Dublin. [*In preparation.*

CAPTIVI. Edited by A. RHYS SMITH, late Junior Student of Christ Church, Oxford. [*In preparation.*

Pliny.—LETTERS. BOOK III. Edited by Professor JOHN E. B. MAYOR. With Life of Pliny by G. H. RENDALL, M.A. 5*s*.

Plutarch.—LIFE OF THEMISTOKLES. Edited by Rev. H. A. HOLDEN, M.A., LL.D. 5*s*.

Polybius.—HISTORY OF THE ACHÆAN LEAGUE. Being Parts of Books II., III., and IV. Edited by W. W. CAPES. M.A. [*In the press.*

Propertius.—SELECT POEMS. Edited by Professor J. P. POSTGATE, M.A., Fellow of Trinity College, Cambridge. Second Edition, revised. 6s.

Sallust.—CATILINA AND JUGURTHA. Edited by C. MERIVALE, D.D., Dean of Ely. New Edition, carefully revised and enlarged, 4s. 6d. Or separately, 2s. 6d. each.

BELLUM CATULINAE. Edited by A. M. COOK, M.A., Assistant Master at St. Paul's School. 4s. 6d.

JUGURTHA. By the same Editor.   [In preparation.

Sophocles.—ANTIGONE. Edited by Rev. JOHN BOND, M.A., and A. S. WALPOLE, M.A.   [In preparation.

Tacitus.—AGRICOLA AND GERMANIA. Edited by A. J. CHURCH, M.A., and W. J. BRODRIBB, M.A., Translators of Tacitus. New Edition, 3s. 6d. Or separately, 2s. each.

THE ANNALS. BOOK VI. By the same Editors. 2s. 6d.

THE HISTORY. BOOKS I. AND II. Edited by A. D. GODLEY. M.A.   [In preparation.

THE ANNALS. BOOKS I. AND II. Edited by J. S. REID, M.L., LITT.D.   [In preparation.

Terence.—HAUTON TIMORUMENOS. Edited by E. S. SHUCKBURGH, M.A. 3s. With Translation, 4s. 6d.

PHORMIO. Edited by Rev. JOHN BOND, M.A., and A. S. WALPOLE, B.A. 4s. 6d.

Thucydides. BOOK IV. Edited by C. E. GRAVES, M.A., Classical Lecturer, and late Fellow of St. John's College, Cambridge. 5s.

BOOKS I. II. III. AND V. By the same Editor. To be published separately.   [In preparation. (Book V. in the press.)

BOOKS VI. AND VII. THE SICILIAN EXPEDITION. Edited by the Rev. PERCIVAL FROST, M.A., late Fellow of St. John's College, Cambridge. New Edition, revised and enlarged, with Map. 5s.

Tibullus.—SELECT POEMS.   Edited by Professor J. P. POSTGATE, M.A.   [In preparation.

Virgil.—ÆNEID. BOOKS II. AND III. THE NARRATIVE OF ÆNEAS. Edited by E. W. HOWSON, M.A., Fellow of King's College, Cambridge, and Assistant-Master at Harrow. 3s.

Xenophon.—HELLENICA, BOOKS I. AND II. Edited by H. HAILSTONE, B.A., late Scholar of Peterhouse, Cambridge. With Map. 4s. 6d.

Xenophon.—CYROPÆDIA. BOOKS VII. AND VIII. Edited by ALFRED GOODWIN, M.A., Professor of Greek in University College, London. 5s.

MEMORABILIA SOCRATIS. Edited by A. R. CLUER, B.A., Balliol College, Oxford. 6s.

THE ANABASIS. BOOKS I.—IV. Edited by Professors W. W. GOODWIN and J. W. WHITE. Adapted to Goodwin's Greek Grammar. With a Map. 5s.

HIERO. Edited by Rev. H. A. HOLDEN, M.A., LL.D. 3s. 6d.

OECONOMICUS. By the same Editor. With Introduction, Explanatory Notes, Critical Appendix, and Lexicon. 6s.

*** *Other Volumes will follow.*

CLASSICAL LIBRARY.

(1) **Texts,** Edited with **Introductions and Notes,** for the use of Advanced Students. (2) **Commentaries and Translations.**

Æschylus.—THE EUMENIDES. The Greek Text, with Introduction, English Notes, and Verse Translation. By BERNARD DRAKE, M.A., late Fellow of King's College, Cambridge. 8vo. 5s.

AGAMEMNON, CHOEPHORŒ, AND EUMENIDES. Edited, with Introduction and Notes, by A. O. PRICKARD, M.A., Fellow and Tutor of New College, Oxford. 8vo. [*In preparation.*

AGAMEMNO. Emendavit DAVID S. MARGOLIOUTH, Coll. Nov. Oxon. Soc. Demy 8vo. 2s. 6d.

SEPTEM CONTRA THEBAS. Edited, with Introduction and Notes, by A. W. VERRALL, M.A., Fellow of Trinity College, Cambridge. 8vo. [*In the press.*

Antoninus, Marcus Aurelius.—BOOK IV. OF THE MEDITATIONS. The Text Revised, with Translation and Notes, by HASTINGS CROSSLEY, M.A., Professor of Greek in Queen's College, Belfast. 8vo. 6s.

Aristotle.—THE METAPHYSICS. BOOK I. Translated by a Cambridge Graduate. 8vo. 5s. [*Book II. in preparation.*

Aristotle.—THE POLITICS.   Edited, after SUSEMIHL, by R. D. HICKS, M.A., Fellow of Trinity College, Cambridge.   8vo.
[*In the press.*

THE POLITICS.   Translated by Rev. J. E. C. WELLDON, M.A., Fellow of King's College, Cambridge, and Head-Master of Harrow School.   Crown 8vo.   10s. 6d.

THE RHETORIC.   By the same Translator. ,   [*In the press.*

AN INTRODUCTION TO ARISTOTLE'S RHETORIC. With Analysis, Notes, and Appendices.   By E. M. COPE, Fellow and Tutor of Trinity College, Cambridge.   8vo.   14s.

THE SOPHISTICI ELENCHI.   With Translation and Notes by E. POSTE, M.A., Fellow of Oriel College, Oxford.   8vo. 8s. 6d.

Aristophanes.—THE BIRDS.   Translated into English Verse, with Introduction, Notes, and Appendices, by B. H. KENNEDY, D.D., Regius Professor of Greek in the University of Cambridge. Crown 8vo.   6s.   Help Notes to the same, for the use of Students, 1s. 6d.

Attic Orators.—FROM ANTIPHON TO ISAEOS.   By R. C. JEBB, M.A., LL.D., Professor of Greek in the University of Glasgow.   2 vols.   8vo.   25s.

SELECTIONS FROM ANTIPHON, ANDOKIDES, LYSIAS, ISOKRATES, AND ISAEOS.   Edited, with Notes, by Professor JEBB.   Being a companion volume to the preceding work. 8vo.   12s. 6d.

Babrius.—Edited, with Introductory Dissertations, Critical Notes, Commentary and Lexicon.   By Rev. W. GUNION RUTHERFORD, M.A., LL.D., Head-Master of Westminster School.   8vo.   12s. 6d.

Cicero.—THE ACADEMICA.   The Text revised and explained by J. S. REID, M.L., Litt.D., Fellow of Caius College, Cambridge.   8vo.   15s.

THE ACADEMICS.   Translated by J. S. REID, M.L.   8vo. 5s. 6d.

SELECT LETTERS.   After the Edition of ALBERT WATSON, M.A.   Translated by G. E. JEANS, M.A., Fellow of Hertford College, Oxford, and Assistant-Master at Haileybury.   8vo. 10s. 6d.
(See also *Classical Series.*)

Euripides.—MEDEA.   Edited, with Introduction and Notes, by A. W. VERRALL, M.A., Fellow and Lecturer of Trinity College, Cambridge.   8vo.   7s. 6d.

Euripides.—IPHIGENIA IN AULIS. Edited, with Introduction and Notes, by E. B. ENGLAND, M.A., Lecturer in the Owens College, Manchester. 8vo. [*In preparation.*

INTRODUCTION TO THE STUDY OF EURIPIDES. By Professor J. P. MAHAFFY. Fcap. 8vo. 1s. 6d. (*Classical Writers Series.*)

(See also *Classical Series.*)

Herodotus.—BOOKS I.—III. THE ANCIENT EMPIRES OF THE EAST. Edited, with Notes, Introductions, and Appendices, by A. H. SAYCE, Deputy-Professor of Comparative Philology, Oxford; Honorary LL.D., Dublin. Demy 8vo. 16s.

BOOKS IV.—IX. Edited by REGINALD W. MACAN, M.A., Lecturer in Ancient History at Brasenose College, Oxford. 8vo. [*In preparation.*

Homer.—THE ILIAD. Edited, with Introduction and Notes, by WALTER LEAF, M.A., late Fellow of Trinity College, Cambridge. 8vo. Vol. I. Books I.—XII. 14s.

THE ILIAD. Translated into English Prose. By ANDREW LANG, M.A., WALTER LEAF, M.A., and ERNEST MYERS, M.A. Crown 8vo. 12s. 6d.

THE ODYSSEY. Done into English by S. H. BUTCHER, M.A., Professor of Greek in the University of Edinburgh, and ANDREW LANG, M.A., late Fellow of Merton College, Oxford. Fifth Edition, revised and corrected. Crown 8vo. 10s. 6d.

INTRODUCTION TO THE STUDY OF HOMER. By the Right Hon. W. E. GLADSTONE, M.P. 18mo. 1s. (*Literature Primers.*)

HOMERIC DICTIONARY. For Use in Schools and Colleges. Translated from the German of Dr. G. AUTENRIETH, with Additions and Corrections, by R. P. KEEP, Ph.D. With numerous Illustrations. Crown 8vo. 6s.

(See also *Classical Series.*)

Horace.—THE WORKS OF HORACE RENDERED INTO ENGLISH PROSE. With Introductions, Running Analysis, Notes, &c. By J. LONSDALE, M.A., and S. LEE, M.A. (*Globe Edition.*) 3s. 6d.

STUDIES, LITERARY AND HISTORICAL, IN THE ODES OF HORACE. By A. W. VERRALL, Fellow of Trinity College, Cambridge. Demy 8vo. 8s. 6d.

(See also *Classical Series.*)

Juvenal.—THIRTEEN SATIRES OF JUVENAL. With a Commentary. By JOHN E. B. MAYOR, M.A., Professor of Latin in the University of Cambridge. Second Edition, enlarged. Crown 8vo. Vol. I. 7s. 6d. Vol. II. 10s. 6d.

Juvenal.—THIRTEEN SATIRES. Translated into English after the Text of J. E. B. MAYOR by ALEXANDER LEEPER, M.A., Warden of Trinity College, in the University of Melbourne. Crown 8vo. 3s. 6d.

(See also *Classical Series*.)

Livy.—BOOKS I.—IV. Translated by Rev. H. M. STEPHENSON, M.A., Head Master of St. Peter's School, York. [*In preparation*.

BOOKS XXI.—XXV. Translated by ALFRED JOHN CHURCH, M.A., of Lincoln College, Oxford, Professor of Latin, University College, London, and WILLIAM JACKSON BRODRIBB, M.A., late Fellow of St. John's College, Cambridge. Cr. 8vo. 7s. 6d.

INTRODUCTION TO THE STUDY OF LIVY. By Rev. W. W. CAPES, Reader in Ancient History at Oxford. Fcap. 8vo. 1s. 6d. (*Classical Writers Series*.)

(See also *Classical Series*.)

Martial.—BOOKS I. AND II. OF THE EPIGRAMS. Edited, with Introduction and Notes, by Professor J. E. B. MAYOR, M.A. 8vo. [*In the press*.

(See also *Classical Series*.)

Pausanias.—DESCRIPTION OF GREECE. Translated by J. G. FRAZER, M.A., Fellow of Trinity College, Cambridge.

[*In preparation*.

Phrynichus.—THE NEW PHRYNICHUS; being a Revised Text of the Ecloga of the Grammarian Phrynichus. With Introduction and Commentary by Rev. W. GUNION RUTHERFORD, M.A., LL.D., Head Master of Westminster School. 8vo. 18s.

Pindar.—THE EXTANT ODES OF PINDAR. Translated into English, with an Introduction and short Notes, by ERNEST MYERS, M.A., late Fellow of Wadham College, Oxford. Second Edition. Crown 8vo. 5s.

THE OLYMPIAN AND PYTHIAN ODES. Edited, with an Introductory Essay, Notes, and Indexes, by BASIL GILDERSLEEVE, Professor of Greek in the Johns Hopkins University, Baltimore. Crown 8vo. 7s. 6d.

Plato.—PHÆDO. Edited, with Introduction, Notes, and Appendices, by R. D. ARCHER-HIND, M.A., Fellow of Trinity College. Cambridge. 8vo. 8s. 6d.

TIMÆUS.—Edited, with Introduction and Notes, by the same Editor. 8vo. [*In the press*.

PHÆDO. Edited, with Introduction and Notes, by W. D. GEDDES, LL.D., Principal of the University of Aberdeen. Second Edition. Demy 8vo. 8s. 6d.

PHILEBUS. Edited, with Introduction and Notes, by HENRY JACKSON, M.A., Fellow of Trinity College, Cambridge. 8vo. [*In preparation*.

Plato.—THE REPUBLIC.—Edited, with Introduction and Notes, by H. C. GOODHART, M.A., Fellow of Trinity College, Cambridge. 8vo [*In preparation.*]
THE REPUBLIC OF PLATO. Translated into English, with an Analysis and Notes, by J. LL. DAVIES, M.A., and D. J. VAUGHAN, M.A. 18mo. 4s. 6d.
EUTHYPHRO, APOLOGY, CRITO, AND PHÆDO. Translated by F. J. CHURCH. 18mo. 4s. 6d.
(See also *Classical Series.*)

Plautus.—THE MOSTELLARIA OF PLAUTUS. With Notes, Prolegomena, and Excursus. By WILLIAM RAMSAY, M.A., formerly Professor of Humanity in the University of Glasgow. Edited by Professor GEORGE G. RAMSAY, M.A., of the University of Glasgow. 8vo. 14s.
(See also *Classical Series.*)

Polybius.—THE HISTORIES. Translated, with Introduction and Notes, by E. S. SHUCKBURGH, M.A. 8vo. [*In preparation.*]

Sallust.—CATILINE AND JUGURTHA. Translated, with Introductory Essays, by A. W. POLLARD, B.A. Crown 8vo. 6s.
THE CATILINE (separately). Crown 8vo. 3s.
(See also *Classical Series.*)

Studia Scenica.—Part I., Section I. Introductory Study on the Text of the Greek Dramas. The Text of SOPHOCLES' TRACHINIAE, 1–300. By DAVID S. MARGOLIOUTH, Fellow of New College, Oxford. Demy 8vo. 2s. 6d.

Tacitus.—THE ANNALS. Edited, with Introductions and Notes, by G. O. HOLBROOKE, M.A., Professor of Latin in Trinity College, Hartford, U.S.A. With Maps. 8vo. 16s.
THE ANNALS. Translated by A. J. CHURCH, M.A., and W. J. BRODRIBB, M.A. With Notes and Maps. New Edition. Cr. 8vo. 7s. 6d.
THE HISTORIES. Edited, with Introduction and Notes, by Rev. W. A. SPOONER, M.A., Fellow of New College, and H. M. SPOONER, M.A., formerly Fellow of Magdalen College, Oxford. 8vo. [*In preparation.*]
THE HISTORY. Translated by A. J. CHURCH, M.A., and W. J. BRODRIBB, M.A. With Notes and a Map. Crown 8vo. 6s.
THE AGRICOLA AND GERMANY, WITH THE DIALOGUE ON ORATORY. Translated by A. J. CHURCH, M.A., and W. J. BRODRIBB, M.A. With Notes and Maps. New and Revised Edition. Crown 8vo. 4s. 6d.
INTRODUCTION TO THE STUDY OF TACITUS. By A. J. CHURCH, M.A. and W. J. BRODRIBB, M.A. Fcap. 8vo. 18mo. 1s. 6d. (*Classical Writers Series.*)

Theocritus, Bion, and Moschus. Rendered into English Prose with Introductory Essay by A. LANG, M.A.   Crown 8vo. 6s.

Virgil.—THE WORKS OF VIRGIL RENDERED INTO ENGLISH PROSE, with Notes, Introductions, Running Analysis, and an Index, by JAMES LONSDALE, M.A., and SAMUEL LEE, M.A.   New Edition.   Globe 8vo.   3s. 6d.

THE ÆNEID.   Translated by J. W. MACKAIL, M.A., Fellow of Balliol College, Oxford.   Crown 8vo.   7s. 6d.

GRAMMAR, COMPOSITION, & PHILOLOGY.

Belcher.—SHORT EXERCISES IN LATIN PROSE COM-POSITION AND EXAMINATION PAPERS IN LATIN GRAMMAR, to which is prefixed a Chapter on Analysis of Sentences.   By the Rev. H. BELCHER, M.A., Rector of the High School, Dunedin, N.Z.   New Edition.   18mo.   1s. 6d.

KEY TO THE ABOVE (for Teachers only).   3s. 6d.

SHORT EXERCISES IN LATIN PROSE COMPOSITION. Part II., On the Syntax of Sentences, with an Appendix, includ-ing EXERCISES IN LATIN IDIOMS, &c.   18mo.   2s.

KEY TO THE ABOVE (for Teachers only).   3s.

Blackie.—GREEK AND ENGLISH DIALOGUES FOR USE IN SCHOOLS AND COLLEGES.   By JOHN STUART BLACKIE, Emeritus Professor of Greek in the University of Edinburgh. New Edition.   Fcap. 8vo.   2s. 6d.

Bryans.—LATIN PROSE EXERCISES BASED UPON CAESAR'S GALLIC WAR.   With a Classification of Cæsar's Chief Phrases and Grammatical Notes on Cæsar's Usages.   By CLEMENT BRYANS, M.A., Assistant-Master in Dulwich College. Extra fcap. 8vo.   2s. 6d.

KEY TO THE ABOVE (for Teachers only).   3s. 6d.

GREEK PROSE EXERCISES based upon Thucydides.   By the same Author.   Extra fcap. 8vo.   [In preparation.

Colson.—A FIRST GREEK READER.   By F. H. COLSON, M.A., Fellow of St. John's College, Cambridge, and Senior Classical Master at Bradford Grammar School.   Globe 8vo.
[In preparation.

Eicke.—FIRST LESSONS IN LATIN.   By K. M. EICKE, B.A., Assistant-Master in Oundle School.   Globe 8vo.   2s.

Ellis.—PRACTICAL HINTS ON THE QUANTITATIVE PRONUNCIATION OF LATIN, for the use of Classical Teachers and Linguists.   By A. J. ELLIS, B.A., F.R.S.   Extra fcap. 8vo.   4s. 6d.

England.—EXERCISES ON LATIN SYNTAX AND IDIOM ARRANGED WITH REFERENCE TO ROBY'S SCHOOL LATIN GRAMMAR. By E. B. ENGLAND, M.A., Assistant Lecturer at the Owens College, Manchester. Crown 8vo. 2s. 6d. Key for Teachers only, 2s. 6d.

Goodwin.—Works by W. W. GOODWIN, LL.D., Professor of Greek in Harvard University, U.S.A.
SYNTAX OF THE MOODS AND TENSES OF THE GREEK VERB. New Edition, revised. Crown 8vo. 6s. 6d.
A GREEK GRAMMAR. New Edition, revised. Crown 8vo. 6s.
"It is the best Greek Grammar of its size in the English language."—ATHENÆUM.
A GREEK GRAMMAR FOR SCHOOLS. Crown 8vo. 3s. 6d.

Greenwood.—THE ELEMENTS OF GREEK GRAMMAR, including Accidence, Irregular Verbs, and Principles of Derivation and Composition; adapted to the System of Crude Forms. By J. G. GREENWOOD, Principal of Owens College, Manchester. New Edition. Crown 8vo. 5s. 6d.

Hadley and Allen.—A GREEK GRAMMAR FOR SCHOOLS AND COLLEGES. By JAMES HADLEY, late Professor in Yale College. Revised and in part Rewritten by FREDERIC DE FOREST ALLEN, Professor in Harvard College. Crown 8vo. 6s.

Hodgson.—MYTHOLOGY FOR LATIN VERSIFICATION. A brief Sketch of the Fables of the Ancients, prepared to be rendered into Latin Verse for Schools. By F. HODGSON, B.D., late Provost of Eton. New Edition, revised by F. C. HODGSON, M.A. 18mo. 3s.

Jackson.—FIRST STEPS TO GREEK PROSE COMPOSITION. By BLOMFIELD JACKSON, M.A., Assistant-Master in King's College School, London. New Edition, revised and enlarged. 18mo. 1s. 6d.
KEY TO FIRST STEPS (for Teachers only). 18mo. 3s. 6d.
SECOND STEPS TO GREEK PROSE COMPOSITION, with Miscellaneous Idioms, Aids to Accentuation, and Examination Papers in Greek Scholarship. 18mo. 2s. 6d.
KEY TO SECOND STEPS (for Teachers only). 18mo. 3s. 6d.

Kynaston.—EXERCISES IN THE COMPOSITION OF GREEK IAMBIC VERSE by Translations from English Dramatists. By Rev. H. KYNASTON, D.D., Principal of Cheltenham College. With Introduction, Vocabulary, &c. New Edition, revised and enlarged. Extra fcap. 8vo. 5s.
KEY TO THE SAME (for Teachers only). Extra fcap. 8vo. 4s. 6d.

c

Lupton.—AN INTRODUCTION TO LATIN ELEGIAC VERSE COMPOSITION. By J. H. LUPTON, M.A., Sur-Master of St. Paul's School, and formerly Fellow of St. John's College, Cambridge. 2s. 6d.

LATIN RENDERING OF THE EXERCISES IN PART II. (XXV.-C.). 3s. 6d.

Mackie.—PARALLEL PASSAGES FOR TRANSLATION INTO GREEK AND ENGLISH. Carefully graduated for the use of Colleges and Schools. With Indexes. By Rev. ELLIS C. MACKIE, Classical Master at Heversham Grammar School. Globe 8vo. 4s. 6d.

Macmillan.—FIRST LATIN GRAMMAR. By M. C. MAC- MILLAN, M.A., late Scholar of Christ's College, Cambridge; sometime Assistant-Master in St. Paul's School. New Edition, enlarged. 18mo. 1s. 6d. A SHORT SYNTAX is in preparation to follow the ACCIDENCE.

Macmillan's Latin Course. FIRST PART. By A. M. COOK, M.A., Assistant-Master at St. Paul's School. Globe 8vo. 2s. 6d.   ** *The Second Part is in preparation.*

Macmillan's Shorter Latin Course. By A. M. COOK, M.A., Assistant-Master at St. Paul's School. Being an abridgement of "Macmillan's Latin Course," First Year. Globe 8vo. 1s. 6d.

Marshall.—A TABLE OF IRREGULAR GREEK VERBS, classified according to the arrangement of Curtius's Greek Grammar. By J. M. MARSHALL, M.A., Head Master of the Grammar School, Durham. New Edition. 8vo. 1s.

Mayor (John E. B.)—FIRST GREEK READER. Edited after KARL HALM, with Corrections and large Additions by Pro- fessor JOHN E. B. MAYOR, M.A., Fellow of St. John's College, Cambridge. New Edition, revised. Fcap. 8vo. 4s. 6d.

Mayor (Joseph B.)—GREEK FOR BEGINNERS. By the Rev. J. B. MAYOR, M.A., Professor of Classical Literature in King's College, London. Part I., with Vocabulary, 1s. 6d. Parts II. and III., with Vocabulary and Index, 3s. 6d. Complete in one Vol. fcap. 8vo. 4s. 6d.

Nixon.—PARALLEL EXTRACTS, Arranged for Translation into English and Latin, with Notes on Idioms. By J. E. NIXON, M.A., Fellow and Classical Lecturer, King's College, Cambridge. Part I.—Historical and Epistolary. New Edition, revised and enlarged. Crown 8vo. 3s. 6d.

PROSE EXTRACTS, Arranged for Translation into English and Latin, with General and Special Prefaces on Style and Idiom. I. Oratorical. II. Historical. III. Philosophical and Miscella- neous. By the same Author. Crown 8vo. 3s. 6d.

Peile.—A PRIMER OF PHILOLOGY. By J. PEILE, M.A., Fellow and Tutor of Christ's College, Cambridge. 18mo. 1s.

Postgate and Vince.—A DICTIONARY OF LATIN ETYMOLOGY. By J. P. POSTGATE, M.A., and C. A. VINCE, M.A. [*In preparation.*

Potts (A. W.)—Works by ALEXANDER W. POTTS, M.A., LL.D., late Fellow of St. John's College, Cambridge; Head Master of the Fettes College, Edinburgh.
HINTS TOWARDS LATIN PROSE COMPOSITION. New Edition. Extra fcap. 8vo. 3s.
PASSAGES FOR TRANSLATION INTO LATIN PROSE. Edited with Notes and References to the above. New Edition. Extra fcap. 8vo. 2s. 6d.
LATIN VERSIONS OF PASSAGES FOR TRANSLATION INTO LATIN PROSE (for Teachers only). 2s. 6d.

Reid.—A GRAMMAR OF TACITUS. By J. S. REID, M.L., Fellow of Caius College, Cambridge. [*In preparation.*
A GRAMMAR OF VERGIL. By the same Author. [*In preparation.*
** *Similar Grammars to other Classical Authors will probably follow.*

Roby.—A GRAMMAR OF THE LATIN LANGUAGE, from Plautus to Suetonius. By H. J. ROBY, M.A., late Fellow of St. John's College, Cambridge. In Two Parts. Third Edition. Part I. containing:—Book I. Sounds. Book II. Inflexions. Book III. Word-formation. Appendices. Crown 8vo. 8s. 6d. Part II. Syntax, Prepositions, &c. Crown 8vo. 10s. 6d.
"Marked by the clear and practised insight of a master in his art. A book that would do honour to any country."—ATHENÆUM.
SCHOOL LATIN GRAMMAR. By the same Author. Crown 8vo. 5s.

Rush.—SYNTHETIC LATIN DELECTUS. A First Latin Construing Book arranged on the Principles of Grammatical Analysis. With Notes and Vocabulary. By E. RUSH, B.A. With Preface by the Rev. W. F. MOULTON, M.A., D.D. New and Enlarged Edition. Extra fcap. 8vo. 2s. 6d.

Rust.—FIRST STEPS TO LATIN PROSE COMPOSITION. By the Rev. G. RUST, M.A., of Pembroke College, Oxford, Master of the Lower School, King's College, London. New Edition. 18mo. 1s. 6d.
KEY TO THE ABOVE. By W. M. YATES, Assistant-Master in the High School, Sale. 18mo. 3s. 6d.

Rutherford.—Works by the Rev. W. GUNION RUTHERFORD, M.A., LL.D., Head-Master of Westminster School.
A FIRST GREEK GRAMMAR. New Edition, enlarged. Extra fcap. 8vo. 1s. 6d.

Rutherford.—Works by the Rev. W. G. RUTHERFORD, M.A.,
(*continued*)—REX LEX. A Scientific Etymology for Use in
Schools. 8vo. [*In preparation.*

THE NEW PHRYNICHUS; being a Revised Text of the
Ecloga of the Grammarian Phrynichus. With Introduction and
Commentary. 8vo. 18*s*.

Simpson.—LATIN PROSE AFTER THE BEST AUTHORS.
By F. P. SIMPSON, B.A., late Scholar of Balliol College, Oxford.
Part I. CÆSARIAN PROSE. Extra fcap. 8vo. 2*s*. 6*d*.
⁎ *A Key to the above for Teachers only. Extra Fcap. 8vo*, 5*s*.

Thring.—Works by the Rev. E. THRING, M.A., Head-Master of
Uppingham School.

A LATIN GRADUAL. A First Latin Construing Book for
Beginners. New Edition, enlarged, with Coloured Sentence
Maps. Fcap. 8vo. 2*s*. 6*d*.

A MANUAL OF MOOD CONSTRUCTIONS. Fcap. 8vo. 1*s*. 6*d*.

White.—FIRST LESSONS IN GREEK. Adapted to GOOD-
WIN'S GREEK GRAMMAR, and designed as an introduction
to the ANABASIS OF XENOPHON. By JOHN WILLIAMS
WHITE, Ph.D., Assistant-Professor of Greek in Harvard University. Crown 8vo. 4*s*. 6*d*.

Wright.—Works by J. WRIGHT, M.A., late Head Master of
Sutton Coldfield School.

A HELP TO LATIN GRAMMAR; or, The Form and Use of
Words in Latin, with Progressive Exercises. Crown 8vo. 4*s*. 6*d*.

THE SEVEN KINGS OF ROME. An Easy Narrative, abridged
from the First Book of Livy by the omission of Difficult Passages;
being a First Latin Reading Book, with Grammatical Notes and
Vocabulary. New and revised Edition. Fcap. 8vo. 3*s*. 6*d*.

FIRST LATIN STEPS; OR, AN INTRODUCTION BY A
SERIES OF EXAMPLES TO THE STUDY OF THE
LATIN LANGUAGE. Crown 8vo. 3*s*.

ATTIC PRIMER. Arranged for the Use of Beginners. Extra
fcap. 8vo. 2*s*. 6*d*.

A COMPLETE LATIN COURSE, comprising Rules with
Examples, Exercises, both Latin and English, on each Rule, and
Vocabularies. Crown 8vo. 2*s*. 6*d*.

Wright (H. C.)—EXERCISES ON THE LATIN SYNTAX.
By Rev. H. C. WRIGHT, B.A., Assistant-Master at Haileybury
College. 18mo. [*In preparation.*

ANTIQUITIES, ANCIENT HISTORY, AND PHILOSOPHY.

Arnold.—Works by W. T. ARNOLD, M.A.
A HANDBOOK OF LATIN EPIGRAPHY.   [*In preparation.*
THE ROMAN SYSTEM OF PROVINCIAL ADMINISTRA-
TION TO THE ACCESSION OF CONSTANTINE THE
GREAT. Crown 8vo. 6s.

Arnold (T.)—THE SECOND PUNIC WAR. Being Chapters of
THE HISTORY OF ROME. By the late THOMAS ARNOLD,
D.D., formerly Head Master of Rugby School, and Regius Professor
of Modern History in the University of Oxford. Edited, with Notes,
by W. T. ARNOLD, M.A. With 8 Maps. Crown 8vo. 8s. 6d.

Beesly.—STORIES FROM THE HISTORY OF ROME.
By Mrs. BEESLY. Fcap. 8vo. 2s. 6d.

Classical Writers.—Edited by JOHN RICHARD GREEN, M.A.,
LL.D. Fcap. 8vo. 1s. 6d. each.
EURIPIDES. By Professor MAHAFFY.
MILTON. By the Rev. STOPFORD A. BROOKE, M.A.
LIVY. By the Rev. W. W. CAPES, M.A.
VIRGIL. By Professor NETTLESHIP, M.A.
SOPHOCLES. By Professor L. CAMPBELL, M.A.
DEMOSTHENES. By Professor S. H. BUTCHER, M.A.
TACITUS. By Professor A. J. CHURCH, M.A., and W. J.
BRODRIBB, M.A.

Freeman.—HISTORY OF ROME. By EDWARD A. FREE-
MAN, D.C.L., LL.D., Hon. Fellow of Trinity College, Oxford,
Regius Professor of Modern History in the University of Oxford.
(*Historical Course for Schools.*) 18mo.   [*In preparation.*
A SCHOOL HISTORY OF ROME. By the same Author.
Crown 8vo.   [*In preparation.*
HISTORICAL ESSAYS. Second Series. [Greek and Roman
History.] By the same Author. 8vo. 10s. 6d.

Geddes.— THE PROBLEM OF THE HOMERIC POEMS.
By W. D. GEDDES, Principal of the University of Aberdeen.
8vo. 14s.

Gladstone.—Works by the Rt. Hon. W. E. GLADSTONE, M.P.
THE TIME AND PLACE OF HOMER. Crown 8vo. 6s. 6d.
A PRIMER OF HOMER. 18mo. 1s.

Jackson.—A MANUAL OF GREEK PHILOSOPHY. By
HENRY JACKSON, M.A., Litt.D., Fellow and Prælector in Ancient
Philosophy, Trinity College, Cambridge.   [*In preparation.*

Jebb.—Works by R. C. JEBB, M.A., LL.D., Professor of Greek in the University of Glasgow.

THE ATTIC ORATORS FROM ANTIPHON TO ISAEOS. 2 vols. 8vo. 25s.

SELECTIONS FROM THE ATTIC ORATORS, ANTIPHON, ANDOKIDES, LYSIAS, ISOKRATES, AND ISAEOS. Edited, with Notes. Being a companion volume to the preceding work. 8vo. 12s. 6d.

A PRIMER OF GREEK LITERATURE. 18mo. 1s.

Kiepert.—MANUAL OF ANCIENT GEOGRAPHY, Translated from the German of Dr. HEINRICH KIEPERT. Crown 8vo. 5s.

Mahaffy.—Works by J. P. MAHAFFY, M.A., Fellow and Professor of Ancient History in Trinity College, Dublin, and Hon. Fellow of Queen's College, Oxford.

SOCIAL LIFE IN GREECE; from Homer to Menander. Fifth Edition, revised and enlarged. Crown 8vo. 9s.

RAMBLES AND STUDIES IN GREECE. With Illustrations. Second Edition. With Map. Crown 8vo. 10s. 6d.

A PRIMER OF GREEK ANTIQUITIES. With Illustrations. 18mo. 1s.

EURIPIDES. 18mo. 1s. 6d. (*Classical Writers Series.*)

Mayor (J. E. B.)—BIBLIOGRAPHICAL CLUE TO LATIN LITERATURE. Edited after HÜBNER, with large Additions by Professor JOHN E. B. MAYOR. Crown 8vo. 10s. 6d.

Newton.—ESSAYS IN ART AND ARCHÆOLOGY. By C. T. NEWTON, C.B., D.C.L., Professor of Archæology in University College, London, and Keeper of Greek and Roman Antiquities at the British Museum. 8vo. 12s. 6d.

Ramsay.—A SCHOOL HISTORY OF ROME. By G. G. RAMSAY, M.A., Professor of Humanity in the University of Glasgow. With Maps. Crown 8vo.   [*In preparation.*

Sayce.—THE ANCIENT EMPIRES OF THE EAST. By A. H. SAYCE, Deputy-Professor of Comparative Philosophy, Oxford, Hon. LL.D. Dublin. Crown 8vo. 6s.

Wilkins.—A PRIMER OF ROMAN ANTIQUITIES. By Professor WILKINS, M.A., LL.D. Illustrated. 18mo. 1s.

GREEK TESTAMENT.

Greek Testament.—Edited, with Introduction and Appendices, by CANON WESTCOTT and Dr. F. J. A. HORT. Two Vols. Crown 8vo. 10s. 6d. each.
  Vol. I. The Text.
  Vol. II. Introduction and Appendix.

Greek Testament.—Edited by Canon WESTCOTT and DR. HORT. School Edition of Text. 12mo. cloth. 4s. 6d. 18mo. roan, red edges. 5s. 6d.

Greek Testament.—THE ACTS OF THE APOSTLES. Being the Greek Text as revised by Drs. WESTCOTT and HORT. With Explanatory Notes by T. E. PAGE, M.A., Assistant Master at the Charterhouse. Fcap. 8vo. 4s. 6d.

The Gospel according to St. Mark.—Being the Greek Text as revised by Drs. WESTCOTT and HORT. With Explanatory Notes by Rev. J. O. F. MURRAY, M.A., Lecturer in Emmanuel College, Cambridge. Fcap. 8vo. [In preparation.

School Readings arranged in a Course of Thirty-six Lessons mainly following the Narrative of St. Mark. Edited with Introduction, Notes, and Vocabulary, by Rev. A. CALVERT, M.A., late Fellow of St. John's College, Cambridge. Fcap. 8vo.
                                      [In the press.

The Greek Testament and the English Version, a Companion to. By PHILIP SCHAFF, D.D., President of the American Committee of Revision. With Facsimile Illustrations of MSS., and Standard Editions of the New Testament. Crown 8vo. 12s.

St. John's Epistles.—The Greek Text with Notes and Essays, by BROOKE FOSS WESTCOTT, D.D , Regius Professor of Divinity and Fellow of King's College, Cambridge, Canon of Westminister, &c. Second Edition Revised. 8vo. 12s. 6l.

St. Paul's Epistles.—Greek Text, with Introduction and Notes.

  THE EPISTLE TO THE GALATIANS. Edited by the Right Rev. J. B. LIGHTFOOT, D.D., Bishop of Durham. Eighth Edition. 8vo. 12s.

  THE EPISTLE TO THE PHILIPPIANS. By the same Editor. Eighth Edition. 8vo. 12s.

  THE EPISTLE TO THE COLOSSIANS AND TO PHILEMON. By the same Editor. Eighth Edition. 8vo. 12s.

St. Paul's Epistles.—THE EPISTLE TO THE ROMANS. Edited by the Very Rev. C. J. VAUGHAN, D.D., Dean of Llandaff, and Master of the Temple. Fifth Edition. Crown 8vo. 7*s*. 6*d*.

THE EPISTLE TO THE PHILIPPIANS, with Translation, Paraphrase, and Notes for English Readers. By the same Editor. Crown 8vo. 5*s*.

THE EPISTLE TO THE THESSALONIANS, COMMENTARY ON THE GREEK TEXT. By JOHN EADIE, D.D., LL.D. Edited by the Rev. W. YOUNG, M.A., with Preface by Professor CAIRNS. 8vo. 12*s*.

THE EPISTLES TO THE EPHESIANS, THE COLOSSIANS, AND PHILEMON ; with Introductions and Notes, and an Essay on the Traces of Foreign Elements in the Theology of these Epistles. By the Rev. J. LLEWELYN DAVIES, M.A., Rector of Christ Church, St. Marylebone ; late Fellow of Trinity College, Cambridge. Second Edition Revised. Demy 8vo. 7*s*. 6*d*.

The Epistle to the Hebrews.—In Greek and English. With Critical and Explanatory Notes. Edited by Rev. FREDERIC RENDALL, M.A., formerly Fellow of Trinity College, Cambridge, and Assistant Master at Harrow School. Crown 8vo. 6*s*.

The Epistle to the Hebrews.—The Greek Text, with Notes and Essays, by BROOKE FOSS WESTCOTT, D.D., Canon of Westminster, and Regius Professor of Divinity in the University of Cambridge. 8vo. [*In the press.*